THE PULLMAN HILTON

A CHRISTMAS MYSTERY

CHARLIE RYAN

Single Star ★

A Division of Ovens Onboard, Ltd.

The Pullman Hilton
A Christmas Mystery

Printed in the USA by ArtBookPrinting.com, a specialty markets company of Inner Workings.

Cover Design: Single Star ★

Cover image ©Nils Z from Shutterstock Inc.

Single Star ★ is a registered trademark of Ovens Onboard, Ltd. whose books may be ordered through booksellers or at www.singlestar.us or PO Box 5566, Hilton Head Island, SC 29938 or by calling 843·290·9900.

ISBN: 978-0-9908273-0-6
Library of Congress Control Number: 1172291838

1950026

This story is dedicated to MV—my sister,
Mary Virginia—who was always by my side.

− 1 −

When the snow whips around you and hammers your face like ten-penny nails, you know it's winter. We shivered, but we were determined to press on, trooping through the bitter wind toward an abandoned graveyard. Apprehension was in the air as our destination came into view—silently sleeping in a cover of white—ghostly in appearance.

We climbed platform stairs and pushed open a heavy door, hesitating only briefly as curiosity overcame fear. We advanced tentatively, brushing snow from our heavy jackets, feeling like intruders. Even in the frigid winter day the smell inside was musty, the air heavy.

We were in the belly of an old Pullman railroad car, one of several hundred left to rot on land long neglected. Weeds and wild foliage peeked through the snow beneath the soiled carpeting that covered steel wheels under our feet—wheels that would never again move down a railroad track. The wind chill outside the coach was absent here and nervous perspiration began to soak my shirt and jacket as I sensed a presence of some sort.

Attempting to divert an uneasy feeling that was creeping over me, I counted sixteen windows on each side of the Pullman car, completely covered with grime. I concentrated hard, trying to shake my fear, trying to remain calm, but something—some thing was coming—and going.

My sister, MV, at eleven years of age, was the oldest of our group. She moved down the long, narrow aisle of the car with assurance, demonstrating her seniority to the rest of us, all ten years old. It appeared that I alone was nervous about our surroundings as Randy and Munch poked and prodded at every surface, searching for treasure. Jazz Man softly hummed a Christmas carol. Junior read aloud the signage in the car, right down to the tiny nameplates that bespoke where the car was built and its passenger capacity.

Tank simply struggled to push his muscular frame up the aisle, his overcoat making the passage even more difficult. I followed him and saw only the width of his back as we moved forward. Spiders scurried, awakening from their dormant winter slumber as we waded through the debris that had resided here for years.

This was the fifth car we had explored today. Each Pullman held the promise of something new—lost diamond rings, wallets, luggage—the possibilities were endless. For the moment, however, we had found nothing save a makeup bag some primping lady had discarded or lost, and a pocket-size photograph of a moment in time for an unknown family; a mother and father, a little girl and boy, looking directly at the camera. I paid the photo little attention but it was in good condition and I stuffed the picture in my back pocket.

Randy rifled through a luggage storage area, convinced he would find treasure. "Diddly squat, nothing here," he said, surveying the musty bin. "I'd settle for a rat, just something to stir up the dust." Impatient, he ran his fingers through his blonde, curly hair, shaking his head in frustration.

"Tell you what," Junior muttered, "we better find something that makes this worth the risk. My old man will beat the living daylights out of me if he finds out I was in the Pullman yard."

Without warning, the door at the rear of the Pullman exploded, its rusting metal hinges moaning in protest as a human form hurtled toward us, screaming, heavy-leaden footsteps thundering down the aisle.

The scene played before me in slow motion. I looked at Munch and saw terror in his eyes. Jazz Man turned ever so slowly toward the far end of the car, his horn rim sunglasses hiding his reaction to the pulsating sounds.

We ran, rushing for the opposite door. We jumped from the car, straddling the platform leading to the next Pullman, sliding on ice and metal, terrified by the stentorian sound of boots and blood curdling screams that followed us into the car.

I shot a glance over my shoulder. Bearded man, huge, something in his hand—high pitched howls searing the winter chill. An object whizzed by my head. A knife? I ran faster.

The Maple Avenue Gang shot out of the Pullman, hurtling from its platform, falling into drifts of snow. We regained our footing and fled into the darkening shadows of winter's dusk like human cannonballs.

We covered several hundred yards when I realized MV was not with us.

"Wait, wait!" I yelled.

"No way! Shoot the moon!" Munch yelled, "That crazy giant looked like he was gonna' slit us from ear to ear!"

"He was sure a big'un'—did ya' see him!" Tank yelled at Randy as he continued to sprint toward the alley that led to our houses. "Beard! Ice dripping from it!"

"Wait!" I shouted again, "MV's still back there!"

Munch, Randy, Tank, Junior, and Jazz Man came to a skidding stop, panting hard.

"We left her back there?" Junior asked, his voice climbing to its highest octave.

"Geez, we gotta' get her!" I hissed, turning on my heel, running hard through the snow. Munch and Randy shot each other a worried glance and fell in behind Tank, Jazz Man and Junior who were following me to the Pullman car.

We hopped aboard the car's platform, expecting we would die at any minute. From inside the Pullman we heard a low moan as wind began to whistle through broken windows, spreading white flakes through the air.

"MV!" I cried, seeing my sister sprawled in the aisle, whimpering softly, wind chilling her face.

"Are you alright?" I asked, my voice quivering as I crouched down to whisper in her ear, looking furtively over my shoulder, sensing someone was there, then gone. My eyes made note of a knife that had plunged into the bulkhead at the end of the car.

MV finally responded to my question, nodding her head that she was okay. "Hit my head when I fell," she said, "knocked myself out, I think." She tried to stand, falling as she did so, her hair cascading back over her forehead, revealing a bloody gash across her temple. Tank appeared by MV's side, picked her up and carried her from the car.

A red handkerchief dropped to the floor as Tank walked away. I snatched it from the crusty carpeting, observing it was freshly laundered, soiled only by MV's blood; someone, or, was it some—thing, had used it to try and stop the bleeding.

I looked around once more, feeling a presence, vanishing, reappearing, coming, going. I slowly backed down the aisle, eyes darting throughout the car, and then I turned and fled, running after Tank and my sister. Tank eased her gently into the snow and I knelt at her side, asking if she was hurt.

"I'm okay, I'm okay," she said, "it's freezing out here!"

"You're bleeding," Randy exclaimed as MV brushed her hair back from her forehead.

"He had a knife! He threw it; did he hit you?"

"I think I hit my head on something when I fell," MV said, alert once more as the winter cold brought her wide awake. "It's just a scratch," she said.

"Like heck," I said, cleaning her forehead with snow, showing her the blood on the bandana. I frowned, folding the cloth to its clean side, reapplying it to her forehead, instructing her to keep it pressed firmly against the wound.

"Somebody used this handkerchief to help stop the bleeding," I said.

"Who would have done that?" Tank asked, looking back at the Pullman, shivering in the cold.

"I don't know, but, believe me, somebody—or some thing—is in that car," I said, as all heads turned toward the Pullman.

"Yeah, a bearded guy with a knife," Tank scoffed.

"Right, but, something else, something really strange," I said.

"Let's get outa' here," Junior said, looking furtively over his shoulder, watching for the bearded man. It seemed to us very sound advice. We all began a slow gait, finally bolting, running for home.

"Son-of-a-gun, that was close, pretty cool," Jazz Man said, breaking into nervous laughter as we slowed to a trot. The rest of the gang began to giggle and Tank laughed out loud. I looked back one last time at the abandoned car, feeling eyes following our retreat.

A solitary figure standing in the old Pullman car used the palm of his hand to wipe dirt from the encrusted car's window, watching the Maple Avenue Gang depart. He was ethereal in presence, coming, going, gazing into the swirling snow. The fleeing youngsters before his eyes slowly morphed to thirty years earlier and a scene forever embedded in his memory began to play through his mind. He squinted and brought the vision to life.

Hundreds of travelers scurried about the railroad platform in Washington, D.C. A well-dressed passenger in a heavy overcoat was ushering his wife and two children aboard a luxurious private car on the Baltimore & Ohio Railroad's Royal Blue Line, bound for 89 East 42nd Street in New York City—Grand Central Station. Christmas decorations were abundantly displayed as men, women and children flowed through Washington's Union Station, passing billowing, hissing B&O Baldwin P-7 "President" steam engines, poised to run.

Voices drifted across the decades as a small girl and her brother kept stride with their mother. A conductor shouted "All aboard," his lungs thundering above the Christmas carols and sea of voices—all melding into a roar.

The lone figure in the old Pullman car steadied himself, grabbing the frame of a passenger seat, viewing the visions that played before him, reliving the moment.

"Daddy! Look! Smell!" the girl shouted, entering the car, pointing to staterooms that awaited the family, running to a freshly-made bed, jumping on it, bouncing, delighted with the fragrance of lavender that emanated from the lush bedding.

"Lisa Lee, remember you are a lady," her mother chided, admonishing the giggling girl, smiling as she did so, appreciating the plush surroundings in a private railroad car built for elite travelers who could afford to pay the price to travel in the highest of style.

The girl's brother chimed in, laughing, "Mother, it's Christmas, Lisa Lee's eight today, and spoiled rotten. Next thing we know," the boy said, matching his mother's smile, gathering his sister in one arm, applying a Dutch rub to her scalp and long blonde hair, "she'll be having a holiday cocktail in the lounge."

"I can't wait, Rudy!" the girl shouted, turning, running briskly through the length of the Pullman, "I'm eight today, it's Christmas Eve and Santa comes tomorrow!"

The scene faded and the walls seemed to close in on the tall, elegant black man who stood staring through the window of the abandoned car, watching snowflakes melt through the mist of his tears.

— *2* —

Snow crunched under our feet and freezing temperatures enveloped our little railroad town, turning our cheeks rosy red. It was December 20, 1938, and we were free of school for two weeks, eagerly awaiting Christmas day.

There were seven of us and we called ourselves the Maple Avenue Gang. We lived in the town's North End, across the railroad tracks that bisected our community. It was the latter days of the Great Depression and we knew there would be few Christmas gifts under the tree.

We had elected, therefore, to create a Christmas present to give ourselves. There was little money to finance such a quest, although MV and I each had somehow collected nickels and dimes and were proud to say we had saved $4.25 between us—a munificent sum we thought, given the stringent time in which we lived. We offered the precious coins to our gang, but $4.25 spread among seven of us did not go far. Better, we thought, to create a different gift—an adventure—a gift that would fill our Christmas vacation with excitement and cause us to forget about presents under the tree.

Paddy Town, named for the Irish that had settled there was a railroad town, sure enough, and proud to be so. Population, just under 6,000; I thought of it as a large city. Living in a railroad town during the late days of the Depression with pre-war clouds looming was a lucky break; railroads were essential to the national security and there was more employment in our little town than most.

My sister Mary Virginia was a tomboy, but pretty as a picture, and we were close. She had brown hair, bangs, and a wide smile with freckles dotting her face. In summer we wore tee shirts and blue jeans, or what we called dungarees, not knowing dungarees and blue jeans were made of different materials. In winter we both donned corduroy for additional warmth. Both our "cords" and dungarees had an assortment of patches and were beginning to become too small for our growing bodies.

We played year round with the Palmer, Malone, Sider and Arden kids, who lived down the street. Only Freddy Smiley did not live in the North End. He ventured each day from his home in the East End to join our gang on Maple Avenue. We called him Jazz Man, because, at ten years of age, he played a mean saxophone. He had thick black hair and was a skinny kid with big ears.

Randy Palmer always flashed a crooked smile and he loved to tease. He was a tinkerer—exhibiting an early addiction to automobiles, as did Junior Sider, who regularly had to be ousted from bed to join our group as we began morning forays.

Munch Malone was a shade taller than Randy and had a deep voice that belied his age. It was Munch who organized our games of Cowboys and Indians, insisting we use BB guns and actually shoot at one another. Amazingly, none of us were wounded.

Tank Arden was quite tall and weighed almost 140 pounds— mostly muscle. His passion was World War I and any armament that had been used in that great conflict. Tank was authoritarian, moving with assurance, simply dismissing with a chuckle any fool who disagreed with him. We loved Tank. I was chubbier than the rest of the crew, with large freckles and a cowlick that stood straight up in the crown of my scalp. I loved to eat and Mom's cooking had taken well, adding pounds to my small frame.

The gift we would give ourselves this Christmas vacation of '38, we all agreed, would take us to yet a new level—serious adventure. We vowed we were the "Maple Avenue Gang", swearing allegiance to one another, planning a Christmas vacation fraught with danger.

We determined that the scariest thing we might do would be to venture into the nearby B&O railroad graveyard, property owned by RJ Higgins, the most detested man in Paddy Town. Mr. Higgins had leased the land to the railroad as a depository for wooden Pullman cars that had been pulled out of service, making way for new steel frames. We were aware that the abandoned cars would soon be bulldozed or disposed of in some way because Higgins had won a city contract to use his land as a garbage disposal center. Folks in the North End of town were livid because Higgins was about to immerse us in garbage. Higgins was, therefore, despised.

The ten acres of Higgins' land adjacent to Maple Avenue housed both run-of-the-mill Pullmans and, here and there, custom made cars that had been luxury on wheels, featuring sleeping, living and dining areas. They featured romantic names such as "The Shenandoah" and "The Ambassador", remnants of aristocratic railroad travel dating from the 1800s into the turn of the century.

Our parents had warned us never to approach the Pullman yard. They assured us that snakes, lice, raccoons, and possibly rabid bats were to be found in the abandoned cars. And, they reminded us, there was a hobo camp on the far side of the property. The cars, they said, were surely visited by all sorts of thieves and vagrants.

That cinched it—all hesitancy was swept aside. The Maple Avenue Gang voted in unison that the Pullman car graveyard was the venue of choice for our Christmas vacation of '38.

— 3 —

Sonny Longsten rubbed a three-day growth of beard and took a long pull on a fifth of whiskey. "Lousy way to start the day—let's hope it turns out better than yesterday," he thought, lighting a cigarette, rubbing his eyes, trying to focus in the first hours of dawn, silently cursing the snow and cold.

Then again, he thought, finding the bottle of Old Grand-Dad whiskey two nights ago under a filthy blanket on a boxcar out of Washington, D.C. had at least made his last 24 hours bearable. Sonny was in the process of working his way across five states, heading up from South Carolina aboard trains carrying raw goods to northern industrialized cities in Ohio, Illinois, Michigan, and Pennsylvania.

It was six in the morning when the freight Sonny had hopped began to slow to a leisurely pace as it chugged toward "Z" Tower on the Baltimore & Ohio Railroad line. The serpentine ride snaked through the rail yard as shreds of sunlight crept through the openings of the rolling stock, offering hope that ice gripping the cars in the yard might soon release its hold.

Silent coal gondolas passed before Sonny's eyes as they waited in 100-car lines for helper engines to push them up the nearby seventeen-mile grade, the steepest railroad incline east of the Mississippi. The freight train moved smoothly over the steel rails and Sonny began to survey the area for railroad bulls that might be patrolling the yard.

The lights that bathed the acres of boxcars, baggage cars and tankers revealed the town's name on a sign placed at the outskirts of the burg—Paddy Town. Sonny chuckled at the name and took another drag from his last Lucky Strike, flicking the cigarette butt out of the boxcar, watching the embers sink into the snow.

"Well, I've got to stop somewhere, at least for a while, so it may as well be Paddy Town," he said to himself, sliding from the moving car, clutching a thin jacket to his body. He landed running, slipping momentarily on ice, noting the yard was quite large, with at least thirty tracks crisscrossing more than what must have been seventy acres. Switches that moved trains from one track to another were, he knew, manned both by hand and remotely with "Armstrong" levers thrown from within Z tower in the distance. This morning there were no switches being manually thrown; the ice encrusted yard seemed to be devoid of people, save himself.

Sonny paused and once again swept the yard with his eyes, shivering, making note of a two-story passenger station, its outer lights on, revealing wooden baggage carts piled high with mailbags covered in snow. The panorama featured a freight station, machine shop, car barn, a large storage facility, and a massive Roundhouse where steam engines were placed on a turntable so that they might be serviced.

On the perimeter of the rail yard, streetlights bathed down on the homes of the Maple Avenue Gang, safely tucked beneath warm covers. They snoozed, blissfully unaware this would be a Christmas they would never forget.

A short distance from where Sonny had begun a search for shelter, Bill Ryan climbed down from a Baldwin Q-3 class steam engine that hissed and blew smoke from beneath its giant chassis and massive iron wheels on track 7 in the Paddy Town yards. The B&O Railroad engineer lit a cigarette and shook his head as he saw a man in a thin coat walking alongside a boxcar on track 2.

"Another hobo," he thought, as the shadowy figure vanished into the whipping snow. He sympathized with the plight of such men, but was adamantly opposed to their commandeering private railroad property and putting their lives in danger as they hopped freights.

Bill's long frame stretched back toward the cab of the steam engine. His hand, soiled from the black smoke that blew from the Q-3's smokestacks, snatched his "grip" from the cab's platform. His railroader's suitcase contained a change of clothes for overnight hauls, a thermos bottle and the remains of a lunch that Mabel had packed for him. He pulled the grip from the train and turned toward home.

Bill moved through heavy snow and across four strands of railroad tracks as darkness continued to give way to the morning sun, struggling to break through snow-filled clouds that had settled in during the night. He would easily cover the distance to Maple Avenue within fifteen minutes, nimbly moving over coarse railroad ties, maintaining his balance as he plowed a path through drifts of white powder.

He emerged from between lines of boxcars, and the railroad yard gave way to the North Side of Paddy Town. He smiled to himself as he saw the neat row of snow-covered houses on Maple Avenue, then frowned, thinking it would be a slim Christmas for his children this year.

He was unaware of a lone figure trailing his path.

Sonny Longsten, standing in the shadow of a tanker car, had decided to follow the railroad engineer, hoping he would somehow lead him to a place where he could flop for the day. He would then wait for nightfall to cover his movements and catch another freight, continuing his journey without, he hoped, encountering railroad bulls.

Longsten half-crouched as he followed Bill, keeping a safe distance behind. He saw something looming to his left and came to a stop, turning his head toward a string of abandoned Pullman railroad cars less than a football field away. Sonny whistled softly, anticipating shelter from the wind and snow, the perfect place to hide for the day. He moved toward the rolling stock, thinking of a warm, dry place to lay his head, quickly forgetting the railroad engineer who moved in the opposite direction, across the last of the rails.

Hurrying to cover the distance to safe harbor as the early morning light began its transition toward warmer temperatures, Sonny climbed onto the rear platform of the first Pullman. He hoisted himself aboard the dormant railroad car just as Bill Ryan unlocked the back door at 174 Maple Avenue, stomping his feet to loosen clumps of snow and ice from his heavy shoes.

Sonny kicked open the passenger car door, waited for a cloud of snow to settle, and moved inside. A silky lace landed softly on his face. He wiped away the spider web that lay across the aisle, its gauze enveloping sturdy ironwork that held ornately decorated benches in place. The car was partially dark and had a ghostly appearance. The once padded and plush upholstery of the embroidered seats was in steady decay with moth eaten wool sprouting from cushions that had padded the posteriors of thousands of passengers. Globe shaped lights stared down from the ceiling, extending the length of the car, their glow forever silenced.

Sonny reached toward the end of his bindle stick and pulled from the cloth pouch a flashlight, helping to light the interior of the car, creating early dawn shadows. He walked halfway through the Pullman and tensed, sensing a presence of some sort. Fatigue overcame fear and he collapsed on a seat, dousing the light, throwing his feet on the bench facing him. He leaned back and closed his eyes, thankful for some warmth and the escape from howling winds and blowing snow. He was exhausted and quickly fell into a deep sleep.

— 4 —

The silence of heavy slumber was shattered by a loud voice from somewhere in the car. Sonny shook off the last dregs of a foggy dream and then he froze. How long had he been out? Was someone there, or was he still dreaming?

"Who are you?" the shrill, hard voice screamed from the far end of the Pullman. Sonny was instantly alert and coiled for defense, his eyes searching through the filmy curtain of sunlight that now cascaded through the dirt-encrusted windows of the car.

The threatening voice came again, "I said, who are you?"

"Name's Sonny Longsten! I just jumped off a Cannonball and I'm cold, hungry and thirsty!"

Silence.

Sonny waited, sensing danger.

At the end of the car a bearded face and a mop of red hair atop a hulk of a man slowly rose from behind one of the passenger seats.

"Older than I am, must be at least 40—lot bigger than I am—need to be careful," Sonny quickly calculated.

The Beard spoke in an eerie high-pitched voice: "Well, Sonny boy, you're trespassing on my property. That means you have to pay. Whatcha' got to pay with?" the bearded face said, threatening.

"Shirt on my back. Didn't realize I'd find an honest to God railroad executive here, or I would have been better prepared.

"How many of these cow crate sleeper cars 'ya own, anyways?" Sonny asked, looking around, his voice echoing sarcasm.

"Loudmouth jungle buzzard, huh? A Yegg that needs to be cut down to size?" the Beard snarled, moving forward, drawing from his pocket a switchblade knife that snapped to attention and pointed toward Sonny.

"Listen, pal, ain't no Yegg—I don't steal nothin'—just lookin' for a place to spend the night, then I'll be gone."

"Do tell, and what makes you think you can spend the night here 'sted of out there in the bushes and snow, covered with the moon?"

"You act like you own the place, friend, but I doubt you have any paper that says you have a right to be here."

The Beard was moving closer. The enormous head to which the Beard was attached moved downward toward where

Sonny was seated and Longsten tensed for the leap and switchblade he knew was coming. Then, the Beard began to shift slightly upward, revealing marvelously white teeth and the beginnings of a smile.

"Aw, hell's fire—tell 'ya what pal, it's Christmas and Arthur and I could use some meaningful conversation. Wouldn't have any whiskey, would 'ya, punk," the high-pitched voice asked.

Sonny relaxed just a bit and returned the smile, reaching into the cloth tied to the end of his bindle stick as he did so.

"Now, truth is, I lied. I do have more than this shirt on my back. I've got a fifth of Old Grand-Dad, glad to share."

"Tokay Blanket? Now you're talkin', welcome to the Pullman yard, friend, and Merry Christmas," the Beard chortled, pocketing the knife and licking his lips.

The largest fellow Sonny had seen in three states was on him. Sonny involuntarily jerked back, again sensing danger. But it was okay; the enormous paw that appeared before him was open, offering a handshake and a high-pitched welcome.

"Name's Joshua Wenning, but you can call me Josh."

Sonny took the beefy fist and gave a firm shake, his own hand seeming to be caught in a vise. "Sonny Longsten," he said.

"Yeah, already heard. And how's your Grand-Dad, the gentleman in that bottle there?" Josh said, looking at the whiskey bottle in Sonny's possession.

"He's lookin' for a cup—two cups," Sonny said, lifting the bottle high.

"Follow me to the Pullman Hilton for a holiday toddy, my good man," Josh grinned, his voice rising to a higher octave.

Sonny fell in behind the 360 pounds that was leading the way. The two men clambered through the deserted car, making their way to its rear platform, stepping over trash, leaves and snow that had blown through the door of the Pullman. A long row of cars stretched through a field of white before them; the Beard easily swung to the next platform and Sonny followed, struggling to keep pace, slipping on strands of ice.

Ten cars down the line Josh Wenning jumped to the ground, landing softly in the snow, Sonny staying in close pursuit. The two moved across an open expanse of field and then entered a second labyrinth of looming sleeping cars. Josh motioned for Sonny to stay close behind as he deftly grabbed an iron railing and hoisted himself onto the platform of a rotting Pullman castaway. Sonny could just make out part of the faded name that spread above the windows—"Blue Line". Josh inserted a key into the wooden door as Sonny, breathing hard, stood beside him. They entered the car.

Sonny walked through the door of the old Pullman and into a dark corridor that stretched before him. Startled, he rubbed his eyes, trying to believe what he was seeing.

The exterior of the windows that lined the custom-made club, dining and sleeper car were coated with dirt and frozen snow; no one could possibly see through them. The crusty windows hid an interior that belied the outer decaying appearance of the car. A few rays of sunlight from the open car door splashed onto decorative carpeting that spread before him, bifurcating a passageway that featured lavishly appointed bedrooms on either side.

Josh moved forward without commenting, and Sonny, in awe, followed. The two were at the end of the car; it featured bedrooms, a dining, bar, and sitting area. Sonny passed by the bedrooms, looking into each, taking into account beds that folded into the wall and dresser drawers and tables that were strategically placed; it was obvious that expert engineering had utilized every inch of space. Sonny noted fine linens on the beds and fragrances from the washrooms wafted to his nostrils.

"What? What is this?" Sonny asked.

"Pullman Hilton," Josh replied, "this here's a special coach that was hauled on the B&O's Blue Line. Custom built— sleeping, drinking, dining, heating, cooling—you name it, it was all here and we've restored it to look pretty much like it used to. This little lady made lots of runs from Washington to New York and Philadelphia. Just think of the high rollers that put out some big dollars to travel in the Pullman Hilton," Josh said, laughing hard. "I figured old Conrad Hilton himself would be glad to offer this here piece of rolling stock as one of his premiere hotel rooms, so I named this baby the Pullman Hilton." Josh spread his arms wide and shouted to the ceiling, "Yes, indeed, 'Filling the earth with light and warmth of hospitality,' that was old Conrad's theme and that's the slogan I use today to welcome you to the Hilton," Josh said, laughing, shrieking really, out loud.

"Unbelievable! This thing looks like it's crumbling on the outside, but inside—brand new," Sonny whistled, continuing down the corridor toward the bar, Old Grand-Dad in tow.

"Yeah, well, Arthur's mainly responsible for that. But I do my part. I look for work, buy or find grub, bring it back here, eat, and then work on the car. This beauty was a private car—like I said, custom made—rich folks bought them and hitched them on to the back of passenger trains. Pretty neat way to travel and, now, a good place to live. I've been here two years. Truth to tell, this car was in pretty good shape, thanks to Arthur. I take responsibility for security, though," he laughed.

"Security?" Sonny queried.

"Yeah, I whacked around on the outside skin, got rid of the gold trim, did all I could to remove things on the exterior." Josh pointed to a round metal seal at one end of the bar. "Maryland state seal—ripped that off the outside of the car—for some reason the manufacturers liked to do that; put state seals on them, designate where they were made.

"Had to tend to little things like that to make this Pullman look like it was about to rot away; good way to keep busybodies out—make them think the car is about to collapse. Once I did that I went to work inside, finishing up some things for Arthur. Lots of items were broken and I replaced them with pieces that might not be authentic, but they work; check out the bar," Josh said, moving behind gleaming mahogany with aluminum trim.

"Even decorated for the season," Sonny said, smiling, waving a hand at candy canes and strands of green pine branches that were carefully placed throughout the car. At the far end of the room stood a Christmas tree, strands of lights encircling it, giving off a warm glow. Sonny sensed he and Josh were not alone, but he wasn't sure. The feeling seemed to come and go.

"Yeah, well, I always liked to do it up at Christmas. The car originally had Pintsch gas for lighting, steam heat for warmth, even had air conditioning," Josh said, pointing to the car's air conditioning intakes, filters and grilled outlets. "I happened upon a few unguarded generators out there in the B&O's rail yard about six months ago and that's how I power things now. I fire up the generators when the big freights come through—covers the sound.

"Course, I limit the lighting, even those Christmas lights, at night. I've blacked out the windows—can't be too careful. Lighting the whole car at one time is something I don't do. Might not know when a beam of light might creep through a crack in the walls. It'd be a dead giveaway that somebody's home. Wish I could use all the lights at night. Be nice to see what the whole thing would look like with full indirect lighting."

"Indirect lighting?" Sonny thought. "Who is this guy, anyway?"

Josh ran a hand across the mahogany, emitting a small sigh as he did. "I polish this bar every day. Matter of fact, I give tender loving care to all that's in the car. Keeps me busy—but, it does look pretty good, doesn't it? Far cry from the rest of the cars in this big old graveyard," he said with obvious pride, looking from where they stood to the far end of the car.

"Oh, yeah, amazing, amazing," Sonny muttered, taking in the scene. The bar area was surrounded by upholstered chairs and deep, cushioned sofas. Ebony rosewood tables and brass lighting fixtures graced the room. At the far end of the car Sonny saw tables and chairs prepared for dining. Several tabletops featured cards, backgammon, and here and there, books and magazines.

Josh winked, moving with grace as he searched for the appropriate tumblers behind the gleaming art deco bar. His height brought him to eye level with the top of the glass shelving that held an array of crystal. He studied the assortment of glasses for a moment, selected two highball goblets, turned, and placed them on the bar in front of Sonny.

"Surplus of glasses, dearth of canned heat, let alone actual whiskey. Your Grand-Dad is most welcome," Josh grinned.

Sonny set the fifth on the bar, gesturing for Josh to do the honors.

Josh obliged, pouring the whiskey "neat", serving Sonny and lifting his glass in a toast. "Sorry, no ice, but here's to the end of prohibition and the damn Depression."

"I'll drink to that, and Merry Christmas to you, my friend," Sonny said, downing the whiskey.

"Yes, yes, yes, Happy Holidays," Josh said, eyeing the empty glass he held in his hand.

— 5 —

"So, Sonny Longsten, what's your story?" Josh said in his quirky high-pitched voice, walking around the bar, gesturing for Sonny to join him in the sitting area in one of the chairs upholstered in old-gold plush. Sonny dropped heavily into the chair and took in the juxtaposition; Christmas tree; whiskey; table lamps with silk shades; and deep, soft carpeting beneath his soiled and heavily worn boots that, regardless of their wear, far outshone his torn trousers and unwashed wool shirt that badly needed cleaning. Sonny knew his body odor was bad, but he was proud of the fact that he had avoided walking dandruff; he hated lice.

"Home's Tuskegee, Alabama," he began. "One year of college at Alabama Polytechnic Institute in Auburn. Parents were moderately well off. My father worked as a teller in a local bank, gave us a middle-class life, insisted I be the first in the family to go to college. Depression hit and it all went down the drain. Dad lost his job, I had to leave school, couldn't find work, went on the road. And, here I am," Sonny grinned, spreading his arms wide.

"Sonny, don't know why, but I like you," Josh said, leaning forward, large, massive forearms on his knees, grabbing the Old Grand-Dad, holding it aloft. "I propose a partnership. This here fifth of whiskey you've invested gives you some equity in the Pullman Hilton. That'll give you a room to sleep in, shelter from the rain and cold, an equal split of any money we earn, and any food and drink we find. You, me, and Arthur, we'll share and share alike," he said.

"I guess I should say thanks for everything," Sonny grinned, "But, seein' as how you don't own this Pullman car, I guess I'd be sayin' thanks for nothing."

"To the contrary, my good fellow, possession is nine-tenths of the law. Arthur and I are homesteading here, at least until I'm offered a good-paying job, or Mr. Roosevelt walks through the door," Josh responded, leaning his giant head back, roaring with laughter.

"Okay, Josh," Sonny shrugged, figuring Josh was maybe a little crazy. "Equity it is. Now, what's your story?"

"I'm, well, I was, a lawyer. Fresh outta' college I joined a New York firm that specialized in commercial real estate. Had it all—job, girlfriends, parties that never seemed to end. But, end it did; stock market crash came and real estate in New York crashed with it. Took a while for the full effect of the Depression to set in, but after a couple of years lots of clients had dropped out and the work dried up. I was cut from the firm. I wanted to throw out a shingle of my own, but the Depression put a stop to that. So, I decided to bum around for a while to see the country in an unvarnished way."

"How'd you get here?" Sonny asked, pointing at Josh.

"Same as you, by rail. Boxcar accommodations—under the boxcar, actually."

"How long before you found the Hilton?" Sonny inquired further, wondering how someone Josh's size could possibly fit under a boxcar.

"Saw the cars when I got off the rattler. I slept in a Pullman that was in bad shape—lots of vermin. Didn't care, roof over my head. I made do. I explored the graveyard when I wasn't out going door-to-door, looking for work, asking for handouts."

"And then you found this?"

"Well, no, it found me, or Arthur did."

"Arthur?"

Josh took a long breath and then said in that curiously high-pitched voice that belied his size, "I was drawn to the car by someone, or some thing. Car mesmerized me as soon as I saw it. It was in pretty good shape, especially for its age. I moved in and helped Arthur bring the old car back to its glory days, started working on it, helping Arthur. Truth is, I think the Pullman Hilton saved me."

"Every day, and especially at Christmas, I thank the Good Lord who led me here, out of the wilderness—took me right straight to Arthur and gave me a mission when I was down and out. I love the Pullman Hilton, may never leave," Josh said, looking around the opulent setting, reaching again for the Old Grand-Dad bottle, smiling, a twinkle in his eye that reflected the Christmas tree and the shadow it cast as its bulbs burned brightly.

"Okay, time to ask the question—who is this 'Arthur' you keep talking about, where is he?" Sonny asked, looking around.

"Oh, Arthur's here somewhere, he'll show up and we won't even know it," Josh replied.

"Alright, then tell me, Josh, how did you know so quickly that I was in one of the cars—one that's a long way from here?" Sonny asked.

"Easy. I patrol the area most days, sometimes at night or early morning. There's a hobo jungle about ten cars over, nearer the tracks. There's a stream over there and a natural spring where everybody gets water. It's a small jungle, used to be three times the size back a few years. Jackrollers come through the camp from time to time and they steal everything from cigarette and cigar butts to hard-earned cash. Those bums are a real problem and I don't want them finding the Hilton," Josh said.

"So, you were just checking your property line, early morning patrol, when you found me?" Sonny asked.

"Yeah, probably wouldn't have spotted you, except you used your flashlight. Even at the break of dawn, in this abandoned place, a flashlight that moves up and down and all around? It's like a beacon. Dirty windows, all that, a flashlight still might be visible. You'll have to be careful with it," Josh said.

"So, you're constantly threatened by the possibility of a visit by Jackrollers? Afraid someone will find out you're here?" Sonny asked.

"Every day. Good thing is, most of the bulls in the area can't help knowing I'm somewhere in the yard, but they ignore me long as there's no trouble outside this bubble I live in. We're right in the middle of 212 cars. I've counted them many times. No one has come round here except for some kids couple of days ago—and that really worries me," Josh said, frowning.

"Over two hundred cars in this graveyard? You're kidding?"

"Nope, 212, to be precise. And I made the mistake of checking out the very one that attracted seven little brats."

"Brats?"

"Local kids, ten, maybe eleven years old."

"Did they see you?"

Josh looked at the carpet, rubbing his glass, and answered with concern. "Afraid so, just briefly, they were too close for comfort. I heard them, kids laughing and shouting. About thirty cars from here, paying no attention to the fact that it was freezing cold, snow up to your butt. The car they were exploring is in rotten shape, full of drifting snow and ice."

Josh shifted uneasily in his seat. "I thought at first it might be a railroad bull or the local cops or some sort of law enforcement. Then I realized it was kids. Still, scared the heck out of me; they were way too close to the Hilton for my comfort. I decided to take a look, went to the car and sneaked in. I scared them all right; I acted like an ogre, ran after them, screaming bloody murder—don't know why, but I threw my knife. Didn't really throw it at them, just put it in the wall of the bulkhead at the end of the Pullman—wanted to really shake them up," he said.

"So, no one was hurt?"

"Well, not quite. The little gal that was with them slipped and fell, hit her head, knocked her out. Rest of the bunch scattered. I checked to make sure she was okay, pretty little thing. Her head had a cut on it and I took my bandanna and tried to stop the bleeding. I didn't know what to do next. I knew she was okay, but I couldn't leave her there."

"What did you do?"

"Didn't have to do anything, the boys came back to get her. Guess they realized she wasn't with them when they ran away. I heard them coming and hid in the car, watched one of the kids, big kid, tote her out. Took some guts for them to come back. I was pretty scary, I'll bet."

"They came back to get the girl? They didn't spot you?"

"Like I said, I made my presence known, threw the knife, and they scattered. Then I tended to the girl, heard them coming and hid behind the seats. I watched the big kid scoop her up and carry her off. I think she was awake by then. Arthur showed up, he saw it all."

Sonny filled the glasses once more.

"Josh, I don't want to say this is a bad road, but those kids are gonna' go straight to their parents and this place will be swarming with cops any day now—your bubble may burst."

"Don't think so."

Sonny's eyebrows went up. "Why not?"

"The little punks were all talking about how they would get a switching or worse if their parents knew they were in the graveyard. I don't think they'll brag about being here. Arthur agrees with me about that."

"Maybe, but what if they do come back?"

"I've been thinking about that. Arthur says we need some way to keep them from doing that," Josh said.

"We? I hope that doesn't include me," Sonny said, eyebrows raised.

"I'm afraid so, Sonny boy—'we'—remember, you've just become an equity holder in the Pullman Hilton, giving you a roof over your head and, as is the way of the world, new responsibilities," Josh grinned.

"Let's develop a plan, because, if our little visitors get in harm's way, you, Arthur, and I will be checking out of the Hilton; we'll be lucky if we don't end up greasing the tracks," Josh said, slapping his knee, sloshing the whiskey out of his glass.

"Sure could use a little splash of that, Mr. Josh," a gentle voice from behind Sonny said.

"Well, well, here's Arthur," Josh said, turning toward the Christmas tree where a tall black man, resplendent in a uniform of some sort, stepped out of the shadows.

— 6 —

Saturday and the Maple Avenue Gang was on its way to Main Street and the Paddy Town Music Hall for the matinee. The Depression had not been able to kill the movies as people sought make-believe to ease the burden of their austere lives. Our parents somehow found a way to cough up movie money for us at least twice a month, pointing us toward the local motion picture theatre.

Munch led the way with Junior, Tank, and Randy in close stride, a few steps back. MV and I brought up the rear. We wound our way through a lot where RJ Higgins mothballed his Carousel and Ferris wheel through most of the winter, breaking it out only for Paddy Town's Street Bazaar the week of Christmas, weather permitting.

Mr. Higgins' storage buildings would soon be empty and, if temperatures rose, his monster wheel would spin throughout Christmas week, resplendent at the corner of North Davis and Armstrong Streets, next to the railroad tracks. I detested the Ferris wheel and hoped for freezing temperatures.

RJ Higgins was, according to my parents and other adults I had overheard gossiping about him, not a nice man. He was in his sixties, a lawyer who systematically acquired parcels of property throughout Paddy Town. His law practice was secondary to his management of real estate. Many of his holdings had been acquired in the management practice as he bought land at basement bargain prices from clients who had been hit hard by the stock market crash that sparked the Depression. RJ himself had gone "short", my parents said, just before the crash. I wasn't sure what that meant, but folks said it had brought enormous wealth to Mr. Higgins. Mom and Dad said his money only made RJ want more—and more.

We decided to cross the tracks at Higgins' Ferris wheel lot, ignoring the railroad crossing a hundred yards away. When freight cars sat on the rails, blocking our crossing, we simply hopped the cars, a practice our parents repeatedly forbade, warning us we would be in peril if the rolling stock suddenly moved. We thought freight hopping was not dangerous at all, and much quicker than walking all the way to the crossing.

On this day we climbed onto the metal ladder of one of the freight cars, swinging our youthful bodies sideways onto the large metal coupler that connected one car to the next, then swinging sideways once more to the ladder on the other side of the car, finally bounding downward onto the rail bed. This we normally did with ease, having climbed aboard the rolling stock countless times in our journey to school or a Saturday matinee. Today's chore, however, was more difficult as we placed gloved hands on snow-covered steel, hoping not to slip.

We safely hopped the cars and moved on to the lot where Higgins' Ferris wheel would be erected. I picked up my pace to escape thoughts of the lurking wheel as fast as I could, but I could not restrain myself and I looked up, dizzy at the thought of its gondola cars swinging back and forth, then plunging, seemingly weightlessly, to earth.

I frowned as I pictured the gondolas moving and shuddered at the thought of being in one of them. I thought it ironic that Ferris wheels were originally called Pleasure wheels. No pleasure there, far as I was concerned, wondering if RJ Higgins might have acquired his wheel simply to frighten people. That had to be his reason, I thought, knowing how folks felt about him.

It was not lost on MV and the Maple Avenue gang that I had stopped, mesmerized, looking up.

"Old man Higgins is gonna' bring on the wheel, Charlie— Christmas season! You gonna' ride the wheel this year, Charlie, huh?" Munch sneered, laughing, as Tank and Randy leaned over his shoulder, grinning in their most mischievous manner.

"Don't know," I lied, feeling the freckles on my face go beet red. "Guess I'll have to wait and see." Truth was, I had no intention of riding the wheel; last year I actually was hunched down in one of the mechanical monster's gondolas, petrified as it reached the top of its arc, hesitated, and then plummeted to earth in cold winter air. It was all I could do not to scream, and I felt a warm trickle move down my leg. The moment the whirling contraption stopped I rushed from the wheel, not caring that my corduroys were wet, enduring the shame of having peed my pants. The moment was high comedy for our gang and something they would never let me forget.

"Tell the truth, Charlie, you're scared out of your mind to ride that Ferris wheel," Munch said, laughing, throwing his hands in the air in mock fright.

"Am not!"

"Yes, you are," Tank agreed, snickering. "Charlie peed his pants on Higgins' wheel last year! Peed your pants, didn'ja?"

"Did not!" I cried, clenching my fists, denying what they knew to be true, setting off down Armstrong Street, passing the railroad crossing where Shorty, the watchman, sat in his little hut, warming himself near his potbelly stove, checking his watch, waiting for the National Limited. He eyed us warily, knowing we had hopped the cars at Higgins' lot. We spotted Jazz Man, leaving his house, wearing dark sunglasses, his jacket collar turned up, "duck-tail" haircut neatly combed, sauntering up Armstrong Street to meet us. At ten years of age Jazz Man presented quite a figure, always moving with rhythm, regularly getting double takes from adults.

Jazz Man joined us as we waited for traffic at Coffman's Dry Goods Store at the corner of Main and Armstrong Streets. The town's Christmas bunting and holiday lights dangled from streetlights, accenting the winter white. Carols from downtown stores drifted across us and merchant's shovels scraped concrete in an effort to clear snow from their storefronts and sidewalks.

"What's up, man?" Jazz Man asked, "What's the scoop?"

"Charlie's thinkin' about wetting his pants again on old man Higgins' Ferris wheel, Jazz Man," Tank laughed.

I was upset and near tears as a vintage Packard moved out of Bob Bailey's Esso Service Station onto Armstrong Street. Everyone in town knew the car was special.

"Wow! Dr. Ward's Packard DeVille!" Junior exclaimed, pointing Randy toward a pure white convertible, snow chains gripping its tires. Dr. Ward was making sure he could make his house calls, no matter the weather.

"Hot mamma!" Randy responded, "Convertible, 320 cubic inch straight eight, 135 horses! Must have cost at least $3,000!"

"How do these guys know this stuff," I wondered, thankful for the small diversion, as Munch and Tank continued to merrily inform Jazz Man that I was too chicken to ride the Ferris wheel.

"Let it go, guys, Charlie's not afraid of anything, he's cool," Jazz Man said. "He wasn't afraid of that hobo in the Pullman car and he isn't afraid of Ferris wheels—so there—chill out," Jazz Man added, stomping his foot in an exclamation mark, checking his collar to make certain it was turned up just so, then leading us across the street.

"You're wrong, Jazz Man. Charlie! Old man Higgins is waitin' for you! Look out! The wheel is goin' up, up, up! It's teetering! Swoosh! Down it goes! What's that yellow stuff flyin' through the air? Did Charlie pee his pants?" Tank yelled, running away from MV, Junior, Jazz Man and me, spouting his teasing dialogue as he sprinted past Wilson's Cut-Rate Shoe Store, Romig's Rexall Drug Emporium, and McCoole's Men's Store—a place I visited often to chat with Calvin McCoole, the owner.

"Just wait is right! Let's see if you guys are man enough to go back into the Pullman cars!" I screamed, even louder. My tormentors were half a block away at that point, paying me no attention. Ahead was the Music Hall Theatre marquee that screamed "Hopalong Cassidy"; its red lights reflected brilliantly on snow piled outside Maurice's Department Store. It was not lost on me that RJ Higgins owned the Music Hall, the lot on which Maurice's sat, and the Hub Pool Hall above Maurice's.

Jazz Man, my sister and I paid our five cents each at the box office and walked through the Music Hall doors, feeling a rush of warm air that swept away winter's chill as we climbed the incline of the lobby that led into the theatre. We headed for the refreshment counter where MV bought the largest bag of popcorn the theatre supplied and I, smoldering from the jabs dished out by Tank and Randy, opted for Jujubes. I didn't like Jujubes that much. They were kind of nasty, but rock hard and served a dual purpose; I could eat them—but, more important, they were deadly assault weapons. Jazz Man and Junior both smiled, knowing what was coming.

Munch, Randy and Tank had already found seats on the main floor of the theatre. They were on the right side of the aisle, halfway down the row of seats. I shoved and pushed MV toward the flight of stairs leading to the balcony on the right side of the entryway. We removed our jackets as we walked up fifteen rows of the balcony section, giving us a commanding view of the screen and the kids sitting in the floor seats. Jazz Man and Junior followed.

The Music Hall filled with noise of coming attractions and I opened the Jujubes. I selected one, took careful aim, and let it fly. Tank yelled "Ow!" and his hand slapped the side of his head. Bulls-eye. Jazz Man stifled a laugh. Junior acted as though he did not know me.

Tank turned around and glared, looking for the perpetrator. I stared straight ahead. Seconds passed and Tank again turned his attention to the screen, now featuring Chapter Ten of the Adventures of Zorro serial.

My hand eagerly found the Jujubes box again and I drew out another missile for launch. Pow! This time Munch took a direct hit in the back of the head. He leaned forward, letting out a yell, "Who did that?"

The few adults around Tank, Munch and Randy looked at the trio, "shssssing" them with disapproval while several younger kids snickered and laughed. I watched Zorro through Chapter Ten, the last installment, and then sat patiently while we viewed previews of the serial that would premiere next Saturday, "Jungle Girl". I could not take my eyes off Nyoka, the voluptuous Jungle Girl, depicted as a white woman living in Africa, rather than as an Asian Princess, the way she had been created in novel form.

Hollywood may have been off the mark when it came to being true to the novel's character, but I rather favored Tinsel Town's version of Jungle Girl, seeing as how Nyoka wore only a halter and loincloth. Alas, she soon faded and the feature film began—Hopalong Cassidy Rides Again. While Hoppy saddled up I returned to the business at hand and re-loaded a Jujube. Jazz Man, who never removed his shades, not even in a theatre, shook his head, but he grinned at the same time and moved his hand forward in a sliding manner, indicating that he was "giving me five", the hip way of showing approval. He pointed to Randy.

I took careful aim at Randy's head and launched the third missile with a mighty effort. I threw so hard I lost balance and almost fell from my seat. The Jujube glanced off Randy's shoulder and landed with a thud just behind Tank's ear. It was a twofer! I might have been off the mark a little, but I had struck with power. Tank jumped to his feet like a Jack-In-The-Box and screamed, "Who's doin' that? I'll whip your butt!"

The entire crowd of matinee goers ignored Hoppy, turning toward Tank and his upraised fist. Through the streaming light of the projector that now cast images of old Hoppy and his trusty steed Topper, I saw RJ Higgins making a beeline for Tank, Munch and Randy. Hoppy waived his black ten-gallon hat above his great steed as it reared back on its rear legs, hoisting Hoppy skyward.

Tank, Randy and Munch found their legs at the same time, leaping across a row of seats, running toward the exit door that opened on the back alley near Church Street. They exited with a bang, sliding through snow and cinders with the laughter of a theatre full of kids ringing in their ears.

"Take that," I muttered, watching my tormentors scramble, "Pee your pants!"

Old man Higgins stood at the open exit door, watching the trio flee, not laughing, his beady little eyes mentally recording the scene.

I was tempted to toss the remaining Jujubes at RJ Higgins but Junior, analyzing the situation, shook his head and I held back. It was a smart decision because Higgins turned from the open door and looked directly up at me. Our eyes connected and I knew he had made a mental note of the Maple Avenue Gang.

— 7 —

Sonny Longsten showered and shaved in an improvised compartment Josh had rigged in his Pullman car. Josh explained that he carried water from the spring near the hobo camp on the far side of the car yard almost daily, taking care to avoid as many people there as possible. Two galvanized buckets were toted on each trip to and from the spring. The tank above Sonny's head carried fifty gallons and Josh made sure it was always filled between showers. Josh advised Sonny it took some work, but this was the Pullman Hilton and water service was paramount, winter or summer.

His body clean for the first time in weeks, Sonny fell into bed and slept for ten hours. He awoke to the sounds and smells of breakfast. He salivated as his nostrils filled with the aroma of fried bacon, but lay still for another fifteen minutes, reluctant to leave the luxurious bedding that had been left behind, still pristine, when the Pullman Hilton was retired. Finally, the smell was too hard to resist and Sonny dressed for the day.

"Josh," Sonny said, stepping into the small kitchen that was used to serve the dining car, "you can get a whiff of that for blocks. How do you fry eggs and bacon without somebody taking notice?"

"Like I said, timing is everything. Folks over on Maple Avenue are having their breakfast—eggs and bacon are everywhere, right, Arthur?"

Sonny turned with a start, realizing he and Josh were not alone, seeing for the second time the figure who had appeared from nowhere the night before, now standing behind the polished bar.

Arthur Boreman nodded a gray head featuring kind eyes that smiled in a benevolent way. "That's right, Mr. Josh, Christmas breakfast is in the air, everywhere," Arthur said, grinning broadly as he walked to the table, sat down, and buttered a slice of toast, dipping it into an egg yolk that was sunny side up, sopping the yellow liquid.

"What's your story, Arthur?" Sonny asked, probing for more information now that introductions had been made, noting that Arthur preferred fresh orange juice, black coffee and bacon, fried crisp. Sonny judged him to be at least 6-1, probably 60 years of age, with a deep and cultured voice.

Arthur was wearing a dark blue Pullman porter's coat with brass buttons, accented by a starched white shirt and elegant red necktie. Sonny had seen such uniforms from a distance, as he rode the rails. He studied Arthur, who was indeed a very handsome man.

"Go on, Arthur, tell him all about it. He's an equity owner, has a right to know, so tell him," Josh said.

Arthur frowned, debating with himself, glancing nervously around the car. Then, he made a decision. He began hesitantly. "Well, the fact is, I have a special situation here in the Pullman yard," Arthur said.

"Special?" Sonny asked.

"Yes, special," Arthur said, hesitantly. "It goes back thirty years. I was the porter on this very car we're in—we were on the B&O's Royal Blue Line. It was exciting—this was a custom-built car and only very rich folks could afford it. I was the porter assigned to the car when a wealthy family boarded in Washington on its run up to New York. Christmas Eve, it was, and a little girl and her brother came on board with their mother and father.

"They were a beautiful family. It was the little girl's birthday, she was eight years old that very day. She and her brother had never been on a luxury Pullman and they were so excited—explored every inch of the car. The sounds always come back to me when I think about that day; porters carrying trunks and luggage packed with clothes for the New York winter, the steam engine blowing smoke, the sounds of Christmas carols at Union Station.

"His name, the father, was Hamilton Dresser. I knew who he was because I read every paper the passengers left on the car. *New York Times, Washington Post, Philadelphia Inquirer,* you name it, our passengers brought all the major papers on board, read them, and left them. Mr. Dresser was featured in many of those papers. He was a renowned architect and had amassed a fortune. He was determined to show his family one of the great cities of the world, a city to match their home in the nation's capital. It was Christmas, and he wanted them to experience a holiday in New York City."

Arthur stopped talking and reached a large hand toward a crystal glass of fresh orange juice on a starched tablecloth. He lifted the glass and drank, wiping his lips with a starched white napkin, leaning back in his chair, lost in thought.

"Yes? So?" Sonny said, pleading to hear more.

"It was between Cumberland, Maryland and Martinsburg, West Virginia that it happened. I was simply worn out. All of us porters worked four hundred hours a month and we were lucky to catch three or four hours sleep during the day; we were supposed to stay awake during the night to make sure the white folks, the passengers, were safe and sound in their beds. I tell you, getting only three hours sleep a night and working those hours will get to a man," Arthur said, emitting a long sigh as pictures from years ago flashed through his mind.

"It must have been about three in the morning. I was slumped over a chair at the end of the car, back there, back beyond the sleeping quarters, dozing. I felt something move by me and slowly realized the little girl, Lisa Lee, was behind me. I turned and saw her little hands gripping the lever to the door of the Pullman, opening it. Frigid wind swept through the car, washing across my face, bringing me to full consciousness. But before I could react, she was out on the platform—her white nightgown whipping in the wind and snow, cold—cold."

Sonny tensed, waiting for the rest of the story.

"I charged out of my chair and rushed out there to get her," Arthur said, tensing, his voice going low, his frame sagging. "Before I could get there her nightgown had caught in the coupler and pulled her down. By that time I was on the platform, grabbing for her; I got her hand. I will never forget her eyes as she slipped from my fingers and disappeared beneath the car—she, she, was swept under the wheels. She never uttered a sound," Arthur said, drumming his fingers on the table where he sat, a thousand-yard stare on his face.

"She was killed?" Sonny asked, not wanting to believe what he had just heard.

"Most certainly was," Arthur said, a frown on his face. "I followed her down but I didn't see her until later, even when the wheels moved over me."

"Wait—are you saying—?"

"Yes, that's what he's saying," Josh interjected. "Arthur also was killed that night, right at the end of this car, he and the little girl."

Arthur nodded. "I didn't remember anything after the wheels passed over me except the soulful stare of that little girl. I woke up here in the Pullman Hilton on one of those beds back there. Woke up out of a dream, dreamt I went down on the rails, snow flying, blinding me, glimpses of that little girl moving away from me like a fairy, up and up, through the snow—and then she was gone. Next thing I knew a voice said I had a choice—I could pass on, leave this earthly home—or stay right here—right in this Pullman car and try to atone for my failure. That was thirty years ago and I'm still here."

Josh looked at Sonny and nodded, signaling that he should wait for Arthur to finish. Both men said nothing as Arthur shrugged his shoulders, shuddering, as he remembered that Christmas.

"Trouble was, I was afraid to pass on because I had committed a terrible sin. I don't know why she left the car—curiosity, I guess. I could have saved that girl's life if I had been on the job. My sin, I was certain then, as I am today, would damn me to Hell. I was afraid—still am. So, I decided to stay right here, right here in the Pullman yard where I woke up—in this abandoned Pullman car. As long as I stay here I know I'll be safe and sound, protected here.

"The fact is, I have not atoned for my dreadful sin and I don't know if I'll go to Heaven or Hell if I venture out of the yard. I'm in purgatory here and I'm too much of a coward to leave," Arthur said, eyes cast downward toward the plush carpeting that surrounded his highly polished black shoes.

Sonny looked at Josh and asked, eyebrows lifting as he pointed at Arthur, "Is he telling me he's a ghost?"

"Don't know what he is. Sometimes he's here, sometimes he's gone, just like that," Josh said, snapping his fingers. "All I know is he tried to save the little girl—did his job. But he disagrees. He thinks he was guilty of sleeping when he wasn't supposed to—dereliction of duty that cost a life. He's told me that many times—the girl might have lived if the porter on the Blue Line car had been awake, taking care to make certain his passengers were in no harm. Like he said, he's certain he'll pass on if he ever leaves the Pullman yard—doesn't know if he'll go up—or down," Josh said, pointing skyward and then down, toward the floor.

Sonny turned to look once more at Arthur, but he was gone. Gone without a sound.

"Yes, it's true," Josh said, seeing Sonny's disbelief, "he just comes and goes. I sure can't figure it out."

Sonny shook his head, not knowing what to believe.

— 8 —

"Here's the way I play it," Josh said, plowing through the snow as his boots moved toward Maple Avenue. "I knock on the door and hold my cap in my hand. I look down as the door is answered; by the way, always go to the back door, and travel the alleys. I try to look as pathetic as I can. When the door is answered I always hope for the lady of the house. She'll say, 'Yes? Can I help you?' Don't say anything at first, and then stutter as you answer.

"Say something like, 'ma'am, I'm down on my luck, I'm cold and I've been on the road a while. Truth is, I, I could use some work and somethin' to eat. I, I'm terrible sorry to bother ya' ma'am, but, well, it's hard to ask, but, it's Christmas and anythin' ya' can spare, it'd be most 'preciated. I don't want somethin' for nothin'; I wanna' work to earn my keep. Is there anythin' ya' need done 'round here?' Then, you look up and into her eyes with the best plea you can project."

"Contractions—nothin', somethin'—you only speak that way

when you're pretending to be a dumb hobo. It's disingenuous to say the least," Sonny said.

Josh slapped Sonny on the back. "That's what I like. A hobo who says 'disingenuous'. Listen, don't use that vocabulary in the alleys. You'll get bounced down the street faster than you can say re-elect Herbert Hoover."

"I'm not sure I'm up to this," Sonny frowned.

Josh stopped abruptly and turned to Sonny. "I felt the same way until my stomach told me it was used to food. Listen, buddy, there's no regular work to be had. Lord knows I've tried to find anything that'll put food on the table. It ain't there, pal. I've gotten past the low esteem, the ridicule some folks throw, and the fear I'll never again amount to anything. Offer me a regular job—somebody—and I'll jump at it. But, for now, my job is to ask for the kindness of others and any piddling little chore I can perform. I'll do that before I'll steal."

"What about the generator, the eggs, the clothes, the soap, the decorations? You stole all that and probably lots of other things."

Josh's eyes narrowed, looking down at Sonny. "I mean really steal, buddy." Josh's face projected anger and then changed abruptly, his red beard parting in a smile, voice at a high pitch. "Those things I took I just stumbled on. No one was holding those things, no one was claiming them. They were just there and I helped myself to the good Lord's beneficence."

"Okay, I recognize rationalization when I hear it, just tell me, where do we start? Is there just madness or a methodology to this?"

Josh ignored the sarcasm, rubbing his beard as they walked toward an alley. "There you go again; 'Rationalization, methodology,' you're going to have to tone it down, bub."

"Sure 'nuff, just pitch me the tutorial," Sonny said.

Josh looked sideways at Sonny. "Remember Sonny boy, nobody likes a smart mouth. This is a small town with God-fearing people. I respect them and so should you. I try to spread the load my requests might put on them in these hard times—so I've tried to work the town from East to West. Now I'll work my way, our way, North to South."

"Once we cover the entire burg, we can begin again. Or maybe by that time FDR will have jobs for us. In any event, just so we have a quick path back to the Hilton, in case you do something stupid, I've picked Maple Avenue, right in our back yard; need to be careful though, the little punks that crashed the bubble might be here."

"Isn't Maple Avenue a little close for comfort? We're only a few alleys from the Pullman yard, somebody might see us coming and going," Sonny said.

"Absolutely, you're right—I've avoided Maple up to now precisely because it's close," Josh replied. "But, since you're in training, and I don't know how you'll work out, Maple Avenue makes sense—easy to get here, easy to get back if you blow your audition." Josh's grin grew larger, causing his ears to pop out even more from his giant head.

"Josh, a question—you're a lawyer. You probably could make a professional living just about anywhere. Why not hang out

48

a shingle somewhere?" Sonny asked.

Josh's face darkened and he shook his head, snow falling from his eyebrows. "No way, the legal profession, short as it was for me, left a bad taste in my mouth. Besides, I don't know if I'd be any good. I've been on the road for a while and things change. I don't think of myself as a lawyer anymore, I think of myself as an educated bum. Kinda' like it, too—something I know I'm good at," he said, smiling once more.

As the two hoboes sauntered forth, making their way to our street, my mom was in the kitchen, making dinner on a cold winter's day. MV and I were playing Chinese checkers, chattering about whether we'd receive any Christmas presents. Our cat, a large Tabby named "Hamnose", curled around our feet.

"Hamnose" Simmons, a B&O brakeman on one of Dad's turns, had found the cat in a caboose two years earlier and tried to find a home for him. Dad took the cat from Hamnose, so named by the railroaders because of Simmons' large proboscis, and carried him home to us. He brought the cat out from behind his back as he entered the house and said to MV and me as we ran to greet him, "Here's Hamnose!"

I moved a marble into a carefully diagnosed position and reached down, stroking Hamnose until he began to purr like a motorboat. MV immediately addressed my move, jumping the marble and three more. I took my time studying my next move and our conversation slowly morphed to the Pullman graveyard. We were still keenly aware that The Maple Avenue Gang had not ventured back to the Pullman yard in two days. We told ourselves we were not really scared, just gathering courage for the next foray.

A knock on the screen door on the back porch got our attention and MV and I ran to the kitchen to see who was there. Mom was first at the door and we stood behind her. She was looking at a very large man with a red beard. A second man stood several steps back, hat in hand.

Mom opened the door, but the screen door remained locked. The wind blew through the kitchen and snow blasted across the porch.

The bearded stranger was looking at the floor, addressing our mom, who held the screen door in place. "Howdy ma'am," our visitor began in a shrill voice, raising his head only slightly, quickly looking down again. "I, I, just wondered, would you happen ta' have any work for me and my buddy here? We're down on our luck this Christmas and we'd 'preciate anything at all so we could maybe work for somethin' to eat and, well, anything at all."

"Are you to be trusted?" Mom asked.

"Yes ma'am, we're honest men, shy of a dollar and short of a meal," the bearded man said, smiling.

MV tugged at my sleeve, trying to say something. I hushed her.

"Well, I could use some help with the washing machine down in the basement. Real mess, water's in the tub and..."

"I could take care of that ma'am," the hobo behind the big man said.

"Oh?"

"Yes ma'am, I know about washing machines."

MV tugged again, harder this time. I ignored her.

"I could give you dinner and some food, but I don't have any money to pay you; my husband handles the…" Mom said, stopping short when she realized she might have just informed the two men that my dad was not home.

"That'd be real kind of you, ma'am. Where's the washer?"

"Go round to the side of the house, I'll let you in through the cellar door."

MV practically tore my arm from my shoulder,

"Mary Virginia, Charlie, you stay put here in the kitchen."

Mom clambered down the stairs that led off the kitchen and to the landing where the door to the basement was.

"Charlie!" MV hissed, "I think the guy with the beard is the hobo that ran after us in the Pullman car."

I was startled at first, and then I assured MV she was imagining things. "Naw, don't think so, these two are real friendly, don't seem like the type to chase girls and throw knives."

The men scraped snow from their shoes and suddenly were in the house, moving down the stairs to the basement. MV and I crept to the landing where we could see and hear the exchange between Mom and the hoboes without being detected.

"Looks like a belt problem, ma'am," the smaller fellow said. "I'll check the tension—looks like it's slipping, won't take long."

"Well, I'll leave you be while I fix dinner," my mother said, smiling for the first time since the knock on the screen door.

"Much obliged, ma'am," the big fellow said.

"He's the guy," MV whispered. "He threw the knife, I know it."

I looked at the big red beard. MV might be right, I thought, mostly because I knew she was generally always right.

I looked at her and whispered back, "Lattice Works."

Mom turned to the stairs to retrace her steps to the kitchen and MV and I quickly ran back up the steps and out the back door and through the snow before she could see us. We went to the front of the house and shoved the lattice gate under the front porch, pushing it open through the snow, and entered. The area under the porch was our hideout and it had warmth from the house above. The area was a conference center and general all around meeting place for the Maple Avenue Gang. We had named it the "Lattice Works".

The space was fairly large, encompassing the footprint of the porch and living room above. It held lots of stored items. Dad used the area as a home for our old lawn mower, snow shovels, garden hose and various rakes, a pick axe and items that remained from his project the summer before: a walkway from the house through the backyard to the alley where we had placed our hands in the soft concrete and entered the year "1937".

"What'll we do, I know that's the guy that chased us," MV said, hunkering down on the dirt floor as I latched the gate behind us, shivering only slightly.

"Well, they seem mighty friendly," I responded.

MV scowled, "Until they throw a knife atcha'—do you think Mom's okay? Do you think we should go find the gang and see what they think?"

"We'll do that, but later. Right now we need to make sure Mom is safe. Let's check 'em out," I said, unlatching the lattice gate, pushing MV out the opening, proceeding around the house and slipping quietly through the cellar door. We could hear our mom clanging pots in the kitchen as we took our positions, creeping closer to the cellar landing ledge, looking down at the two hoboes, one seated on a small bench, the other leaning over the washing machine. Both men had discarded their jackets and had their sleeves rolled up.

"Yep, got a 'B' size belt here. Difference between the 'A' and 'B' belt is the width. You measure across the outside of the belt—the outside diameter of the pulleys. Gotta' check the tension. Too low and it causes it to slip. Belt won't last long if it does that. Bearings and pulleys don't like it neither," the smaller fellow said, tinkering with the washer.

We froze as Hamnose slithered past us, nimbly moving down the stairs and into the basement where he hopped onto the washing machine. I started to move to rescue Hamnose but MV pulled me back.

"Hell—ohhh!" the shorter hobo said, looking at the cat.

"Looks like we got a foreman on the job," the large bearded fellow chortled.

"Guess so, good looking little guy," the smaller hobo said, reaching forward to scratch under Hamnose's chin. "Good kitty, kitty, kitty."

"Nice cat, and nice lady," the big guy said, leaning against the wall, watching his friend cater to the cat, returning to his work as Hamnose strode around the washing machine.

"Yep, and let's hope she's a real good cook," the smaller fellow said.

"She is!" I blurted, slapping my hand over my mouth as soon as I said it.

Both men and Hamnose looked up at the staircase where we hid, startled by my outburst.

"Well, well, look who's here," the big one said, stroking a red beard, feigning a smile.

"You threw a knife at me," MV hissed, voice slightly trembling, but defiant.

"That was you?" the big guy frowned, his eyes narrowing.

"Yes, I knew it was you. I'm gonna' go tell my mom," MV pouted.

"Wish you wouldn't do that, I didn't mean any harm," the red beard said, raising his arms, palms toward MV, in a pleading manner.

"Then whydja' throw a knife?" MV asked.

"Just trying to scare you was all. I'm real sorry. I was afraid you'd tell folks I was in the Pullman yard—that's all. I was afraid somebody would come and kick me out."

"What's your name?" the smaller fellow interrupted, looking at me.

"Charlie, what's yours?"

"They call me Sonny and that's Josh; believe me, we're not going to harm you, neither of us would do that. We're just down on our luck, looking for a place where we can find some food to eat. You and your sister have a real nice warm home, it's Christmas and you should be mighty thankful for all you have."

"I know it's warm. It's warm cause I fire the furnace every morning."

"Don't say?" Sonny grinned, turning to MV.

"What's your name, little lady?" he asked.

"She's MV," I replied.

"Cat got your tongue?" Sonny asked, looking at Hamnose, smiling at MV, finishing his work on the washing machine as it began to gurgle, causing Hamnose to leave his perch and scoot up the steps.

"I'm Mary Virginia, Charlie calls me MV."

"Well, Charlie, MV, mighty glad to meet you. Hope you can keep our little secret about the Pullman car," Sonny said, bringing the washing machine fully to life, his work completed.

"We can do that, but your friend has gotta' promise he won't throw knives," I challenged over the throbbing machine, looking at Josh.

We all broke out in smiles and MV and I giggled way too loudly, just as Mom came down the steps.

"I wondered where you two were. I see you're bothering our visitors—and I see my old washing machine is working again!" Mom gushed. "I can't thank you enough, gentlemen, but it's noon, dinner's ready, and I certainly can feed you pretty well. Come on up to the kitchen," she said, with a sweep of her arm.

— 9 —

All five of us climbed the stairs and found the table set for dinner. Josh and Sonny sang our praises, assuring Mom we had not bothered them as they repaired the washing machine. We beamed with pleasure; chests puffed out, friends to hoboes.

Mom had fried chicken, mashed potatoes and gravy, half runners, and sweet tea, all laid out in fine southern style.

"Don't fix dinner like this all the time, times are hard. When I do this kind of thing it's usually at supper—but it is Christmas and I thought we'd have something that'll hold you boys for a while. I am mighty grateful you came along," Mom said, smiling and motioning for all to sit.

I climbed on a chair and started to reach for the food.

"Charlie—mind your manners and wait for the prayer. Please, gents, have a seat. Charlie, you over there, Mary Virginia, here, by me."

Mom bowed her head and said a Christmas prayer, thanking God for the food on our plates and the divine intervention that fixed her washer. She asked the good Lord to bless our home and the visitors in it and went so far as to ask that Josh and Sonny find their way and always have food for their bodies and love in their hearts for their fellow man. I thought she was simply swell with her prayer, but I kept one eye open, moving from the food on the table to the hoboes sitting there, both with eyes closed and heads bowed.

"Amens" were said all around and I reached for a drumstick as the big fellow with the beard said, "Merry Christmas and may God bless us all."

Mom slapped my hand from the drumstick.

"Charlie. Guests first."

I pulled back and said, "Dad's really gonna' hate it that he missed this dinner."

"Charlie, quiet, speak when spoken to," Mom said, barely controlling her irritation with me.

No doubt about it, our guests now knew for certain the man of the house was not home.

"What's your husband do, ma'am?" Josh asked, his beard dripping of gravy as he wolfed down the food.

Knowing these two men she had never laid eyes on before today were sitting here with a woman and two children who were defenseless, Mom elected to show bravado.

"He's a railroad engineer, mighty fine man, strong man, loves his family, should be home any moment now."

"Gee, Mom, he just left this morning," I said, wondering how he could get to Grafton and back in three hours.

"Charlie, please. I think the caller said your dad was needed for a 'turnaround', should get him back here soon," Mom said, smiling at me, but showing something different in her eyes.

"You're very lucky ma'am, railroad engineers have kept their jobs and they are mighty admired. It's a job anyone would aspire to, 'specially during the Depression," Sonny said, working on a chicken leg.

"Well, it's in the family, the kids' Granddad—Bill's dad—was on the road too.

"Pop—we always called Bill's dad 'Pop', went back on the road during the World War and ran an engine when the B&O couldn't fill the cabs—too many boys off to war. I just hope we don't have a second war, what with all that's going on overseas, that man Hitler and all."

"Pop, that was his name?" Josh asked.

"Actually, the railroaders all called him 'Paddy'—Paddy Ryan. Lots of 'em call Bill that too—the Irish, 'ya know."

Mom hesitated and then asked the question; "What about you fellows? Where are you from?"

"And why are you hoboes?" I asked.

I thought Mom was going to backhand me, but she just stared intently and warned, "Charlie, don't ever ask people personal questions such as that."

"But, Mom, you asked where they're from."

Sonny stepped in. "Don't worry, ma'am, boy's got a right to ask that question, don't he, Josh?"

"Same question I'd ask," Josh agreed, downing a fork full of half runners, grinning.

"I'll tell you 'bout Sonny—he loved fixin' your washin' machine. He's all about tinkerin' with mechanical things, tells me he thought about a degree as a mechanical engineer. Even went to college for a short time."

"What happened?" Mom asked, looking at Sonny who noted that Josh was continuing the façade, once again using contractions in his speech.

Sonny hesitated, looking down at his plate. "Uh, things just sort of fell apart when the stock market crashed back in the twenties and the Depression hit. Hard times started and my folks couldn't afford to keep me in school."

"So," he said, moving his chair back from the kitchen table, drumming his fingers on his knee as Hamnose hopped on his lap, "I jumped a freight in the Auburn rail yards and started my journey, looking for work wherever I could find it.

"I got into repairing mechanical things down in North Carolina when I fixed a tractor broken down in a field alongside the railroad tracks. Since then I've worked my way through at least five states. Along the way I met lots like me. They say as many as two million hoboes are ridin' the rails—boxcars on every railroad lined with men who've lost their jobs and families. Young girls with babies clinging to their hips, no joy in their lives."

We sat silently, contemplating Sonny's travels, as the sound of metal clashed on metal in the distance, echoing the movements of "helper" locomotives pushing boxcars toward the seventeen-mile grade. A slow drip in the kitchen sink, a winter wind howling and the purring of Hamnose were the only other sounds in the room.

Politely, Mom looked at Josh and said, "What about you?"

Josh laughed and said, "Lawyer, ma'am, used to do property law. 'Fraid there's very little property bein' exchanged these days. That's why I'm glad Sonny and I have our hands to fall back on—hands for fixin' things."

— 10 —

I pushed away from the table and gave MV a glance. "Mom, could I be excused? I always had to say that when I left the table. "MV and I want to go play."

"Take your plates over to the sink. You can play after you help me clean up here."

"Nuts," I thought and began the task of removing the dishes with MV's help. I complained to MV, out of earshot of the adults sitting at the table, that Mom never asked us to do dishes after dinner.

"Idiot," she whispered to me, "Mom doesn't want to be here alone with the hoboes."

"Oh," I said, never once thinking Mom might be in harm's way. I slowed my dishwashing duties to a crawl, keeping an eye on Sonny, for whom I now had great respect; Sonny was a warrior of the road. Josh? He was just a lawyer.

I could not wait to tell Munch, Tank, Jazz Man, Junior, and Randy about our encounter with the hoboes from the yard.

"Ma'am, we can't thank you enough. This was mighty kind of you and I'm full as a tick. Is there anythin' else we can do 'fore we move on?" Josh said, wiping his mouth with a napkin, shoving his chair away from the table, standing.

"Same here, ma'am. Can't tell you when I last ate like that. Mighty fine food, mighty fine family," Sonny said, gesturing toward the sink where MV and I toiled at a snail's pace.

"You boys are most welcome—and if you are serious about doing some more work, well, there is one more thing."

"You just name it, ma'am," Josh said, tugging his trousers up.

"You see the kennel out there where we keep the hound dogs?" she asked, pointing toward the kitchen window and the backyard kennel my dad had built for our two hunting dogs, King and Queenie.

"The kennel needs cleaning out and new straw put in the dogs' beds—keeps 'em warm in this cold. I hate to ask you to do that, weather and all, but if you wouldn't mind, I'd sure appreciate it."

"Not at all, we'll do it right now. Do the dogs bite? Are they friendly?" Josh asked in high octave.

Mom laughed again. "They wouldn't hurt a flea. They chase rabbits round to us when we're hunting, but I don't think they'd hurt the rabbit even if they were ever to catch him."

She hesitated.

"Course, if anyone tried to harm me or the kids they'd fly off the handle for sure, probably go for somebody's throat."

Josh and Sonny looked at one another and smiled, knowing Mom still was a bit wary of them.

"Don't doubt it, ma'am, and good for them," Josh said, pulling on his jacket as Sonny did the same. I noted that both their garments were patched and soiled in places.

"Thank you again, you've made this a special day for my friend and me," Josh said, a warm smile on his face. Sonny nodded in agreement and added his thanks. The two men donned their jackets, moved toward the back door, pushed the screen door open, and walked off the porch toward the dogs' kennel.

Well, I was ecstatic. I usually got the job of cleaning the kennel and I hated it in the winter cold. Picking up dog poop was not my idea of fun anytime of year, but I particularly detested it when I was freezing my butt off. I figured these guys would never be back if they had to scoop poop in winter. I quickly finished my dishwashing and pulled on my parka and sauntered out in the yard to watch somebody else do the job I abhorred.

"Scoopin' poop's a tough job, ain't it?" I asked, peering into the kennel at Josh and Sonny, gloved hands at my side, a smile on my already chilled and reddened face.

"Older you get, son, the more of this stuff you'll shovel, we're used to it," Sonny said, grinning at me, expertly gathering the brown leavings into a dust pan kept just outside the kennel door, trooping through the snow to empty the droppings into an old garbage can next to the alley.

That wasn't what I wanted to hear, so I changed the subject.

"Can MV and I come over for a visit?" I asked, nodding my head toward the Pullman graveyard.

Josh stopped in the middle of a straw deposit and looked at me, his eyes narrowing. "Guess so, but you and your sister have to promise you won't tell anyone you're in the yard, and you need to stay away from any hoboes you see, lessen it's me and Sonny," Josh said.

"Can we bring the Maple Avenue gang? That's me and MV and our friends," I explained.

"The kids that were in the Pullman with you?" Josh asked.

"Yep, we got the whole Christmas vacation to explore."

"Don't think so, be better if it's just you and your sister."

"Nope, can't do it. We swore a blood oath we'd stay together, through thick and thin," I said.

"Blood oath—pretty serious," Josh said, looking at Sonny. "So you think you can trust your gang?"

"Trust them? I trust them implicitly," I said.

"Implicitly? Wow, pretty big word for such a little guy," Sonny said, whistling slowly.

"Library," MV said, who had, unbeknownst to me, joined our group, standing just behind me.

"Library?" Sonny said, looking quizzically at MV and then back to me.

My reddened face turned even more scarlet, blood rushing to my temples, embarrassed.

"Yeah, he goes to the library most every day, rides his bike over. Library's in the basement of the yellow grade school, across from Grace Methodist Church," MV said.

"I like the library because it's cool in the summer, warm in winter, not just cause I like to read," I said, stomping my foot.

"Sounds like you're reading some pretty high falutin' books," Josh grinned.

"Guess so. Anyway, you can trust us, all of us," I shot back.

"Tell you what," Sonny said, glancing at Josh and back at MV and me, "Do you have a whistle?

"Whistle? Yeah, I've got a whistle in my bedroom dresser drawer," I answered, starting to shiver in the cold.

"Good. Bring it with you when you come. We'll use that as a signal. Tomorrow, say ten in the morning, you come to the far end of the Pullman yard where the path crosses over to the nearest railroad track. When you get there blow that whistle three times and wait for Josh or me. Give us ten minutes or so. If we don't show, that'll mean there are folks other than Sonny and me movin' around in there and you could get hurt. Don't go in the yard if we don't show. Deal?"

"I guess so, but why do we have to blow the whistle, why can't we just meet?"

"Do what I say. If we don't meet you, come back the following morning, same time, and blow the whistle again," Sonny said.

"Okay," MV jumped in, "we'll do it."

"Good!" Sonny said, winking at Josh, finishing the kennel job, pleased they might have a plan to ensure that the Maple Avenue gang would not disclose the Pullman Hilton.

— 11 —

MV and I were on a mission. We had scrimped and saved and $4.25 was burning a hole in our pockets. We decided to make Christmas purchases at Grayson's Sporting Goods Store for Dad and Murphy's Five and Dime Store for Mom. We didn't know what we would buy, but we were excited to go shopping and left our house early, shortly after eight in the morning.

The snow had been cleared from the town's streets and we mounted our bikes and flew down Maple Avenue, engaged in conversation about our decision to spend our savings. I loved the feel of the smooth glide provided by my Montgomery Ward Hawthorne Zep—a bike second only to the classic Schwinn Camelback that Tank rode. MV and I debiked under the protective canopy of an abandoned Sinclair gas station on Main Street, and waited for 9:00, the time Edgel Grayson would open his store. MV and I sat down to once again count our money, discussing what we might purchase. We emptied our pockets and stacked our nickels and dimes into neat piles.

"Lot of money," I said to MV, breaking the silence.

"Yeah, four dollars and change. I hate to part with it," she said.

"Me too, but I'm glad we're spending it on Mom and Dad," I said.

Our conversation ended abruptly as a man emerged from between two large, overgrown pine trees not twenty feet from us. He erupted through a blanket of snow that cascaded from the trees. We knew immediately that his eyes were on our money, stacked on the concrete pedestal of the now dormant gasoline pumps.

The man, obviously a hobo, walked menacingly toward us, kicking snow and emitting a snarled, grotesque sound.

"What's that you got there, kids?" he sneered. His gaunt face featured an ugly scar that stretched from his forehead down the left side of his face, ending just above his mouth. The face was twisted in a smile that resonated anything but humor, causing the elongated scar to vibrate in red.

I froze and it was not caused by the cold weather. This was not good. MV and I were silent; fear immersed my gaze while MV's eyes were defiant.

The hobo leaned over us, reaching for the money on the concrete, his dirty fingernails scraping across the hard surface.

"Well, well, Merry Christmas. Little gal and guy must know how much old Rem here needs a present from Santy Claus!

Much obliged!" he said, scooping up the change.

"No! That's for our parents!" MV yelled, grabbing as many coins as she could, jumping to her feet, striking out at the stranger. I grabbed her, trying to hold her back. She lunged at the hobo and I caught her just in time.

"Let's go, MV, let's get out of here!" I shouted, jumping between her and the hobo, pushing her toward our bikes.

"That's our money!" She protested, pushing back, just as the bum smacked me across the head, sending me flying into a snowdrift. I tumbled onto my back, scraping my right hand hard across a row of icicles hanging from a metal sign that said "High Test-$.12." Blood flew onto the ground and onto my parka.

The stranger stood over me and pointed a finger; "Shouldn't pass the opportunity to help a poor hobo at Christmas," he sneered, "and if you give me any more trouble I'll give you a present—I'll break your arm and smash your bike. Be good little boys and girls and go home to Mama!"

Believing it was better to live to fight another day, I ran for my bike and fled. I looked over my shoulder, watching MV slowly move toward her bike; for a brief moment I feared she was going to drive directly into Scarface. The bum stared at her until she finally rode off. He then gathered up our $4.25, glared at us and disappeared back into the trees.

I waited for MV at the corner of North Main and Maple Avenue.

"Are you okay?" she asked, bringing her bike to a screeching halt, looking at my bloodied hand.

"Yeah, but I'm mad as a hornet!"

Actually, I was almost crying, but held back the tears.

Then MV looked like she was going to cry. I reached out to her and we hugged and both began to cry.

We composed ourselves and headed for the Palmer house where we knew Randy had a garden hose. We opted for the alley route and had to walk our bikes through the snow. The path took us right into the Palmer's back yard where Randy saw us and came running.

"You've got blood all over you, Charlie!" Randy said, "What happened?"

"Some bum—a hobo—he attacked us! He took our money—$4.25," I sniffled.

"Wow. Didja' fight back? Didja' hit him?"

"Well, sort of," I said, full of bravado, replacing fear with the rush of having had an actual encounter with a truly bad guy. "Yeah, yeah, I got him, laid one on him!" I fibbed, as MV rolled her eyes.

"Looks like he got you, too, I mean, you're bleeding pretty bad," Randy said.

"Pretty badly," MV corrected.

"Yeah, that too," Randy said.

MV, ignoring Randy, helped me clean the blood from my hand, wiping the red stains from my parka, expertly wielding the garden hose in the Palmer back yard. She literally coaxed water from the nearly frozen hose, as we explained to Randy we'd been victims of a holdup.

"What are you gonna' tell Mom?" MV asked me.

"Don't tell her anything," Randy said, "It'll just be trouble."

"How do I explain the blood, numbskull?" I asked, sneering.

"Bike wreck, idiot," Randy shot back.

"Stop it, you two!" MV barked. "Randy, we'd have to tell a lie to Mom if we said Charlie wrecked his bike."

"So?" Randy said.

"There's no damage to the Zep, she'd know I didn't wreck the bike." I said.

"Bang in a wheel spoke." Randy said.

"Not on your life! Nobody touches the Zep!" I exploded.

Randy shrugged, taking the hose from MV, turning off the spigot.

"Okay, you fell off a curb, fell on ice, walked into an open manhole, get creative," he snickered.

"I say we level with Mom," MV said, folding her arms, taking a defiant stand.

"MV's right, I could never lie to Mom," I said, looking at the blood on my clothing.

"Boy, you need practice, I can lie to my old man and he'd never know it. My mom might suspect, but I can usually con her just the same. You need to try it, makes life a lot easier," Randy said, winding the hose and looking at Al Palmer at a distance as Mr. Palmer merrily waved at us, hauling slabs of insulation into his garage.

We walked our bikes the short distance home. Mom was in the yard, playfully building a snowman to surprise us.

"Where have you two been?" she asked, scarcely looking at us as she reached for a carrot to create a nose for the snowman.

"Uh, just bike riding," I answered.

"Well, what do you think of Mr. Snowman," she said, smiling, glancing up, catching sight of my hand that was again bleeding. She dropped the carrot and said, "What? What happened to your hand, Charlie?"

"My hand? Oh, well, we were riding our bikes. I just sorta' had a little accident."

"In the house, now. We need to clean that up," she ordered.

Mom grabbed me, leaving the snowman behind, his nose at his feet, hustling me into the kitchen. She yanked my parka off, threw it down the cellar steps to be washed, rolled up my shirtsleeve, and placed my hand in the kitchen sink under running water. She applied soap, cleaning the blood away, sanitizing the wound. She finished her treatment with Mercurochrome and a large Band-Aid.

I kept waiting for the questions. They never came. Mom assumed I had simply fallen from my bike and did not inquire further. MV and I exchanged nervous glances, but did not offer any details. My mom was concerned only with comforting and treating me. Nothing else mattered.

I realized once again how much I loved my mom.

— 12 —

The Maple Avenue Gang entered the Pullman graveyard at precisely 10:00 the following morning. I reached in my pocket and withdrew my metal whistle and lanyard. I put the lanyard around my neck and started to put the whistle in my mouth.

"That'll probably freeze to your lips," Munch said.

"What?" I asked, hesitating.

"You know, put your tongue on anything metal when it's cold out and your tongue will stick to it—might lose part of your tongue, just saying..."

"That's ridiculous," Junior piped up. "The whistle would have to be frozen for that to happen. I agree that metal is a good thermal conductor so if your tongue heat should diffuse quickly toward it, and the whistle were abnormally frigid, your saliva would freeze like glue, a bond would be created with a high tensile strength—spit glue— but it's not that cold, blow away," Junior concluded, smiling.

Leave it to Junior to confuse while educating. I continued to look at the whistle, thinking about my tongue spit frozen to it.

"Enough crap! Gimme that!" Tank yelled, breaking the frozen moment, grabbing the whistle, pulling it and my neck to him, blowing the whistle as hard as he could three times.

"My posit is admirably demonstrated," Junior said.

"Posit—what does that mean?" Munch asked.

"It means his tongue didn't stick, idiot, the whistle wasn't frozen. I was right, as I usually am," Junior said, eyebrows arching, sneer of a grin on his face.

Tank was moving forward with me in tow, laughing. I yanked the whistle from his mouth with a jerk of my head. Tank stopped in his tracks, checked his teeth with his fingers, and glared at me.

We waited in a standoff, my fists curled for a fight. Thankfully, Tank ignored me and the gang grew quiet, listening for Sonny or Josh. Nothing. No sound. Fifteen minutes passed as we shuffled our feet in the snow, thankful that the day had filled with sunshine to warm us, but mumbling with growing disappointment that our two hoboes were not going to show.

"Guess we'll have to come back tomorrow," I said.

"Not me," Tank said, hoisting his barrel-like form in front of us, towering over the group.

"Are we gonna' let some hobo tell us what we can or can't do? We said we were gonna' explore the graveyard this Christmas and that's exactly what I'm gonna' do. You guys can be chicken if you want, but I'm goin' in."

"Tank's right," Munch said, adjusting his glasses, watching Tank forge ahead, leading the charge through a foot of white accumulation.

"No fear, right?" Munch said, head shaking an affirmative answer as he followed Tank through the snow.

The rest of us stood still, afraid to follow, afraid not to.

"But, we promised we'd not go in the yard if no one showed up," I said, weakly.

"No fear," Randy said, echoing Munch.

"Darn right!" Jazz Man said, falling in line.

I looked at Junior for some analysis. He would strategize and I would follow his lead.

MV, seeing me checking for Junior's mind-set, chewed her lip.

Junior spoke, raising his index finger in the air: "We should initiate our exploration. We must, however, make certain we hide any evidence that we were here." MV rolled her eyes as Junior grabbed a fallen branch and began to sweep through the path of snow. He smiled broadly, impressed by his intellect, as we all were, save MV. The branch made little impact on the imbedded footprints we had made but the sunshine, I realized, would do Junior's job within an hour or so.

We half-walked, half-ran through the yard, drifting farther in, sauntering between the cars. The day was warming somewhat and I imagined summer days to come.

"Which one do we wanna' start with?" Randy shouted at Tank, running his hands through icicles that had formed on the bottom of a Pullman car.

"This one," Munch answered for Tank, grabbing a handrail, pulling himself onto the car's platform with a gloved hand. "The 'Potomac'—betcha' lots of famous people rode this one," he said.

We scrambled after him and cautiously entered the car. It was warm with solar power that had permeated the soiled windows. It also was far dirtier than the car we had explored when we had first ventured into the yard. We meandered down the aisle, looking behind and under the seats, finding nothing but dust, debris from earlier visitors, and broken glass.

We moved on, through two more Pullman cars. We finished our search of the third car, "The Pioneer", and Tank ordered us on to car number four. I looked back as we began to file out of the Pioneer and saw MV had lagged behind. She was down on her hands and knees, halfway down the aisle, staring at the interior wall of the car.

"C'mon, MV, let's go," I shouted. She did not budge.

"Tell your sister to move it," Tank commanded.

"Who put you in charge?" Munch scoffed, pushing Tank aside, walking back to MV.

"What is it?" Munch asked.

"There—something's behind the wall," MV said, pointing at the surface under the Pullman's window. Patterns of rain, cold, and heat through many years had caused the paneled veneer to shrink—revealing the outline of something that pressed against the interior wall.

We crowded around, trying to imagine what was behind the Pullman skin.

MV reached forward and pushed against the wall. A 12 x 12 square of wooden surface buckled inward. MV continued pushing with one hand, grabbing a protruding corner of the indentation with the other. She gave a pull and the section dislodged, revealing a compartment that contained a small black leather satchel that looked like the bag Doctor Huffman always carried when he made a house call at our home.

"Well, well. Merry Christmas," Tank laughed. He leaned over MV and grabbed for the small satchel. He snatched it by its leather strap, pulling it out of its hiding place, losing his balance in performing the act, falling on me as I lay prostrate, trying to push MV and Munch aside so I could see what was happening. Tank lost his grip and the satchel flew over our heads and onto the seats behind us where Randy sat. He caught it on the fly.

"Dang it, Tank, watch what you're doin'!" Jazz Man complained.

"Okay, you can grab the next bag we find, smart guy," Tank shot back.

We looked back at Randy who held the satchel like a prize won at the county fair. It was covered with dust, but we could tell it was an expensive item. Two leather straps held the small bag's flap in place. At the end of each strap was a lock, gold in color.

Randy placed our treasure on the floor of the aisle and we all looked at the fine leather that glistened in the daylight. I wiped the valise clean of dust with my hands and unconsciously deposited the dirt on my washed and clean parka, marveling at our find.

"Open it," Tank ordered. Randy removed his gloves and extended a hand to steady the bag, trying the lock latches with his other hand.

"Locked," he said.

"No kidding, Sherlock," Munch guffawed. "We'll need to pry it open."

"With what? Our teeth?" I said, looking around for anything that would give us leverage on the locks.

"Uh, I know, wait a minute," Randy said, setting the valise on one of the Pullman seats, racing back to the car's platform, and down the steps, scrounging beneath the snow. He returned with a big red brick he had spotted when we entered the Pullman, dusting snow and grime from it.

I hesitated. "Naw, that would scar the leather and smash the locks. Bag's too pretty to do that to it," I said. Randy shrugged and tossed the brick down the aisle toward the end of the Pullman car. It landed with a bang, red dust rising.

"Couldn't just lay it down?" I asked.

"Naw, gotta' make a statement," Randy deadpanned, wiping his hands on the fabric of a passenger seat.

"Pay some attention here, idiots," Junior said. "We should get out of here, take the bag with us."

"Junior's right," Jazz Man said. "We can take it to the Lattice Works and decide what to do."

Our fixation on the valise was suddenly shattered as the Pullman door to our right slammed open. At the end of the aisle stood Scarface.

The hair on the back of my neck stood out like a licorice stick as I watched a sadistic grin cross the face of the man who had accosted MV and me.

The man with the large scar began to move forward.

"Give it to me!" he shouted, waving a knife, teetering as he moved down the aisle.

"He's drunk!" Junior shouted, just as the heavy red brick Randy had discarded flew by my head, smashing into the chest of our assailant with a penetrating thud. The man with the scar went down like a sack of flour.

"Run!" Jazz Man shouted and the four of us made little forward progress as we collided with one another in the narrow aisle, Keystone Cops fashion.

The man with the scar was up on his side, reaching for a seat arm to assist his attempt to stand. He screamed at us, rubbing his chest and cursing.

"You little brats! You're dead! Do you hear me? You're dead! Dead!"

We heard him all right. We disentangled ourselves and ran for our lives, jumping from the back of the Pullman, sliding through ice and snow. I grabbed my whistle as I ran, blowing it as loudly as I could in staccato fashion.

We left the yard as fast as we could, running for Maple Avenue. Scarface could be heard, but we did not see him. We had escaped, thanks to brick-throwing Randy. We boys had outdistanced MV, but we could see her at a distance; she was behind us, moving fast and she was okay.

We were in the alley behind Munch's house, breathing hard. Only when I had caught my breath did I remember the satchel.

"Wait! We left the satchel! Son-of-a-gun!" I exclaimed.

"Crap!" Tank said, "All that for nothing."

We pouted our best, not really seeing MV join our circle.

"We've got to get home, Lattice Works," she said, breathing hard.

MV had the satchel. The prize was in her arms. She smiled broadly and we returned the favor. Excitement ran high.

"Great aim with the brick, Randy," Munch said, slapping him on the back.

"Uh, not me, I didn't throw it," Randy said.

"Who did, then?" I asked, looking around. No one claimed the honor, leaving us scratching our heads.

"We've got to get home," MV said, moving toward Maple Avenue.

"Correct—Lattice Works," Junior advised, and we followed MV.

Inside the Pullman car we had abandoned, Scarface gingerly rubbed his chest, bellowing curses, exiting the car in a daze.

Had he looked to the rear of the Pullman he would have seen a tall black man in an ornate uniform silently watching him, shaking his head in disgust, wiping red brick dust from his hands.

— 13 —

We filed into the Lattice Works under our front porch. The snow that had piled up against the lattice gate had now melted and the day was pleasantly warm. Christmas carols from the Philco drifted through the floor above as Mom listened to some radio program and MV placed the bag in the middle of our circle on dirt that served as the floor of our conference room. We sat in silence; each of us imagining what might be inside the satchel, still shaking from the encounter with Scarface.

"That's the same hobo that attacked MV and me," I informed our council.

"No kidding, the one that bloodied your hand at the gas station?" Randy asked.

"Yes—same guy," MV confirmed.

"Ouch, two times—" Junior said.

"Meaning what?" I asked.

"He means things come in threes," Jazz Man replied. "You'll see Scarface again," he warned.

"Not if I can help it," I said, sticking out my lower lip.

"Forget him," MV said, looking at the leather satchel, "what about the bag?"

"How do we open it?" I asked.

"Get some tools from your dad's workbench," Tank ordered.

Tank was a piece of work; he really enjoyed ordering us around, but this time I quickly followed what sounded like a capital idea; my dad's workbench was in the garage. He owned an amazing assortment of tools that would surely provide a way to pry open the locks at the end of each strap that held the flap of the bag in place.

"Good idea," I said, lifting off my haunches and heading for the Lattice Works door.

I sloshed through melting snow and pushed the door to the garage open. The smell immediately engulfed me—wonderful smells that would later in my life always remind me of my dad; motor oil that had oozed into the dirt floor, old tires, various liquids and glues stored neatly on shelves. My eyes swept the workbench where my dad kept meticulous care of the tools and gadgets purchased from Taylor's Hardware Store down on Water Street.

I selected a slip-wrench to grasp the locks and a pair of pliers to twist their mechanism. As an afterthought I grabbed a rubber mallet. Dad was on the road and my calculation was that he would not return until late tonight. I made a mental note of where the items I had borrowed were placed on or above the workbench so I could return them to their correct places, avoiding, I hoped, discovery that they had been moved. My dad knew his tools.

The Maple Avenue Gang gathered round as I re-entered the Lattice Works and placed the tools beside the satchel. I removed my parka as the temperature rose and placed the slip-wrench on one of the locks, using the pliers to achieve a twisting motion, hoping to break the mechanism. It resisted and after several tries, Tank ordered another approach. "Lay it on a rock, bust it with the mallet," he instructed.

Randy ran to the backyard and returned with a flat rock. I lowered the case to its side, reached for my parka and placed it on the rock. I extended the flaps of the bag and lay them on the folded jacket. Perfect. There was a hard surface beneath the folded cloth, but the jacket would absorb the force of the striking rubber mallet. I had a possibility of breaking the locks open without totally smashing them, or harming the fine leather that softly protected the treasure inside.

"Here, let me do it," Tank said, pushing me aside.

"Tank, quit bein' a horse's behind," Jazz Man scowled, pulling Tank back.

"Yeah, Tank, let Charlie do it," MV said.

I regained my composure as Tank relented, scowling. "Get it right, Charlie," he said, convinced that only he had the strength to swing the mallet hard enough to smash the locks.

I took aim and swung. The mallet bounced off metal and rock and recoiled over my shoulder—but I held on.

"Hah," Tank snorted, reaching for the mallet.

I pulled it away from him, took a mighty swing and hit the first lock, and it popped open.

"Yes! Charlie! Home Run!" MV yelled.

Flushed with success I quickly placed the second lock on the rock and let fly once more. The lock resisted and all of us tensed. I struck again, and again. Tank sat there, sneering. My temper got the best of me and the adrenaline flowed as I swung the mallet like John Henry laying rails. The lock gave way.

Cheers all around with the exception of Tank who scowled once again. No matter, the contents of the satchel were now ours to explore.

— 14 —

Seven years before the Maple Avenue Gang discovered the satchel that was now open before them, Miss Harriet Keyser lay dying in her home in Paddy Town. On a Thursday night, at 11:45, an evening punctuated with heavy rain and thunder, she reached for a glass bell on the stand beside her bed and shook it violently, summoning Ralston Bazzle, her longtime chauffeur, from his bedroom just down the hall. Bazzle heard the faint tinkling. He had slept lightly for some time, never knowing when his ailing employer might need him to rush to her bedside, as he now did. He entered the bedroom and knew immediately that Miss Keyser's time was short.

"Ralston, I haven't long to live. I'm dying, you know that I speak the truth, correct?" she said in an authoritative manner, eyes alert, her hands reaching for him.

"Miss Keyser, don't say that," Ralston pleaded, taking her hands in his, comforting her.

"I need your help, Ralston."

"Yes, ma'am, I will always help you."

Miss Keyser instructed Ralston to go to the attic of her house and remove a floorboard located just to the left of the chimney. She told him he would find a small leather satchel there and that he was to bring it to her.

Ralston returned to her bedside a short time later, satchel in hand. He placed it on the bed beside the dying woman.

Miss Keyser placed her hand on the satchel straps and locks and emitted a slow sigh. "Ralston," she said, breathing with obvious pain, "I have reason to believe that RJ Higgins forced me to sign a fake will at Potomac Valley Hospital two weeks ago."

"Fake will? Toward what end?" the chauffeur asked.

Miss Keyser coughed and a rattled sound passed through her. She regained her composure and said, "I was on some mighty strong painkillers when I was hospitalized—RJ came to see me while I was on the pills."

Ralston nodded, intrigued.

"RJ did some legal work for me in the past and he said I needed to sign a piece of paper that had something to do with insurance on my holdings. When the painkillers wore off I was woozy, had a devil of a time getting my mind straight. But, I swear I believe I signed a document with the words Last Will & Testament," Miss Keyser said, tears coming to her eyes.

"Ralston!" she said, pulling him toward her, coughing in spasms. "I think RJ faked a will to convey a portion of my personal property to himself. He's hounded me for years to buy—dirt cheap, mind you, wanted to steal it from me—my property where the old Pullman cars are. He's always wanted to get the land and build something there that will line his pockets."

Reaching for the small leather bag beside her she said, "I want you to take this satchel to my attorney, John I. Robertson, at the law building next to the courthouse, and give it to him and him alone; John I. is a man I will always trust. There's a letter in the satchel that reveals the hiding place of my real Last Will & Testament," Miss Keyser said, the rustling noise again rising in her chest, her eyes slowly closing.

Ralston nodded in agreement just as a tremor rang through the house from the living room below; the front door slammed open and the noise cascaded through the eighteen-room mansion. For a moment the dying woman and her chauffeur thought they had heard thunder; but it was far worse than that.

"Miss Keyser! RJ here! Comin' up ta' see ya'!" called out the voice from the floor below. RJ Higgins headed for the stairs off the foyer of the sprawling house on Mozelle Street and Miss Keyser's eyes opened wide with fright. "Go! Go, Ralston, don't let RJ take the bag," she said. Squeezing Ralston's hand, her body shuddered as she took her last breath, gone from this world.

Tears quickly came to Ralston's eyes and he gently kissed the back of Miss Keyser's hand. He placed her palms across her chest and simultaneously rose from the chair in which he was sitting, dashing out of her room toward the back staircase, just as RJ strode to the top of the front staircase.

"Ralston, stop! Come here!" RJ cried, seeing Ralston flee with his arm around a small satchel he was carrying.

Ralston descended the staircase like a greyhound, out the front door and down the steps to the driveway and Miss Keyser's prized Cadillac V16.

RJ hesitated as he passed Miss Keyser's bedroom. He stopped and stepped back, looking in on her. He knew in an instant she had passed and that the satchel Ralston was carrying might contain what he had come for. RJ ran for the back steps and plummeted down them. Ralston, at the wheel of Miss Keyser's Cadillac, had pulled from the driveway, and was headed pell-mell down Main Street. RJ ran for his Hudson sedan to give hot pursuit, but Ralston and the V16 were long gone.

Ralston knew he had a good lead on RJ but he had no idea what to do with the case Miss Keyser had entrusted to him. He drove frantically across railroad tracks and turned right on Armstrong Street, his mind racing—where could he hide the bag? Rain pelted the big Cadillac as Ralston swept by the Green Lantern restaurant. The chauffeur mentally reviewed Miss Keyser's dying words and an idea crossed his mind—the North Paddy Town property—the Pullman yard would be an excellent place to hide the satchel—in one of the old cars.

Ralston did a fast U-turn, passing the Sugar Bowl, heading back toward Main Street, once more crossing the tracks toward Maple Avenue as thunder began to cascade through the heavens. He went the length of the street and turned left, toward the Pullman yard. He made a quick check in his rearview mirror; RJ was nowhere in sight. The Cadillac's headlights knifed through the wet darkness and played out with eerie shadows between the rows of abandoned cars in the distance. Ralston gave added pressure to the gas pedal of the huge car, advancing toward the yard, cold shivers running down his spine as lightning lit the sky and thunder crashed over Paddy Town.

The Cadillac rolled into the Pullman yard and came to a stop in puddles up to its hubcaps. Ralston reached across the front seat of the car and hurriedly searched for a pencil he knew was in the glove compartment. Finding it, he grabbed the leather satchel beside him, opened it and retrieved Miss Keyser's sealed envelope. He quickly scribbled detailed instructions on its front, addressing the envelope to anyone who might find the satchel. He opened a side pocket of the leather bag and stuffed the envelope inside, at the same time retrieving a small metal key from within the bag. He then locked the satchel's leather straps in place, rolled down the driver's window of the Cadillac and threw the key out the window into nearby bushes.

Perspiration formed on his forehead as he glanced around, looking for any approaching headlights. Seeing none, he rolled up the window and stepped from the idling motorcar into the ensuing downpour. Losing no time, he plunged through ankle-deep water to the nearest Pullman and clambered aboard the car. He shoved the heavy door open, glancing at the nameplate above it that read "The Pioneer" and ran halfway down the aisle, the lights from the Cadillac illuminating the interior of the abandoned rolling stock.

He stopped. Was he alone? Was someone in the Pullman? Ralston felt a presence.

"Hello! Hello, who's there?" Ralston shouted into the empty car, looking frantically from side to side, expecting RJ Higgins to roar into the Pullman yard at any minute. Ralston's shirt was soaked in cold rain and hot sweat. He raised his arm to wipe his brow with his sleeve and he saw it: between seats just to his left—a wall panel had buckled, revealing an open space where something the size of the satchel he held could be inserted.

Ralston took one more look around, convincing himself he was alone. He knelt and placed the small bag in the opening. It fit almost perfectly and with a slight shove was indeed inside the wall. He then worked with the buckled panel, twisting and turning it, until it was installed back in its original place. No one could know the panel had been disturbed unless they looked closely and were on their knees.

Ralston smiled to himself and hurried back to the Cadillac, racing through the torrential downpour. He would alert John I. Robertson in the morning as to the whereabouts of the satchel. He threw the door to the car open, tried to brush rain from his clothes, hit the starter button, and eased in on the clutch, putting the mammoth car in gear. He applied pressure to the gas pedal and picked up speed as he moved toward Main Street. Sheets of rain swept across the Cadillac's windshield; Ralston passed the State Road Garage where rows of bulldozers and end loaders were parked. He did not see an idling Hudson sedan sitting in the entrance, its lights extinguished. Two beady eyes were focused on the Cadillac as the Hudson moved onto the street in pursuit of the V16.

Nearing the top of Knobley Mountain, just outside the city limits, Ralston saw familiar headlights in his rearview mirror. He smiled to himself. Not to worry; RJ might follow him home, demanding to know what he had carried from Harriet Keyser's house, but to no avail; the satchel was safely hidden. Ralston drove steadily forward, unconsciously increasing his speed as RJ closed the gap between the cars. At the last moment, he realized, too late, that RJ was going to try to force him off the road.

Ralston, now traveling at a high rate of speed, whipped his steering wheel hard to the right as RJ drove his sedan straight at the Cadillac. The V16 that Miss Keyser had so prized went into a skid on the wet road; Ralston fought to control the car as it careened forward, finally banking onto two wheels, sliding ever faster on a road made glassy from the heavy rain. He skillfully avoided a precipitous drop over the mountainside and relaxed momentarily only to realize he was not going to avoid a huge oak tree that was speeding rapidly toward him. The Cadillac hit the tree square on with enormous force and Ralston screamed.

RJ brought his Hudson to a skidding stop, jumped from the car, and ran to the Cadillac, pulling the door of the wrecked car open. He looked down and into the lifeless eyes of a bloody Ralston Bazzle slumped over the steering wheel, dead.

RJ lost no time. He quickly searched the interior of the mangled car for the satchel. He then tried to pry the trunk of the vehicle open, to no avail. Flashing red lights appeared, climbing the road to the top of Knobley. RJ ran into the highway, making a show of flagging down the oncoming police cruiser.

Two days later *The Paddy Town Daily News* ran the story on its front page. "Harriet Keyser Dies; Chauffeur Killed In Car Wreck."

"Harriet Keyser," *The Paddy Town Daily News* reported, "was one of our city's most admired citizens who gave, over a lifetime, enormous support and considerable dollars to many good causes in the area. She was a leading advocate for the elderly and the poor and worked tirelessly in the pursuit of excellence in education. She was especially devoted to the

Mineral County Public Library, spending countless hours designing and building a model repository for books."

The full account of the wreck on Knobley Mountain was included in the body of the story that had been carefully related to police by RJ Higgins. *The Paddy Town Daily News* reporter picked it up from the investigating officers and the subsequent review related that local businessman RJ Higgins had happened upon the wreck, shortly after it occurred, while returning home from a late night inspection of his properties. Higgins related that he had rushed through the blinding storm to the twisted frame of the Cadillac, desperately hoping to assist anyone in the car.

Alas, RJ had said, the driver was dead. The newspaper report said police had praised RJ Higgins for his effort, including his insistence that he personally supervise the prying open of the wrecked car's trunk to determine if Miss Keyser had left any valuables that he, RJ, could retrieve for her. None were found. Higgins modestly said of his attention to detail that it was something anyone would have done and he deserved no praise for his selfless attempt to help.

RJ's reward for his deeds that evening was years of sleepless nights, not for his sins, but because of his angst and worry about the whereabouts of the leather satchel that surely held Miss Keyser's original will. Where could it be?

− 15 −

Seven years after the fatal wreck on Knobley, the Maple Avenue Gang sat in the Lattice Works under our front porch, unaware we were answering RJ's question. We formed a circle, looking down at a now unlocked satchel.

Adrenalin flowed through our young bodies following our encounter with Scarface and our hasty retreat from the Pullman yard. The small satchel before us was our prize for placing ourselves in harm's way and we hesitated to violate it. The delay was too much for Tank. He lunged for the bag. Junior grabbed Tank, trying to jerk him back.

"Wait, Tank, hold on a minute, let's take our time. Let's guess what's inside," Junior insisted, as Tank shook him off.

"Yeah, let's just enjoy the moment, might be a genie inside who'll give everybody three wishes" Jazz Man giggled.

MV looked at Randy, rolled her eyes, looked at Tank, and motioned toward the satchel with a nod of her head that suggested we stop the foolishness and get on with the business at hand.

Tank obliged, grabbing the bag again, throwing open the flap and turning the satchel upside down, shaking it furiously.

Nothing. Nothing came flying out.

"Merry Christmas, my foot," Tank said, kicking the dirt floor on which we sat.

He stopped shaking the satchel and looked inside. His face erupted into a smile. He sat the bag on the floor and unbuttoned an interior pocket of the leather case.

We all gathered round, sensing pay dirt. Tank made a show of it, dramatically pulling an envelope, partially damaged by either water or heat from its silk resting place.

"Open it," Jazz Man said.

"Wait," Junior cautioned, looking up at Tank, seeing writing on the front of the envelope, "What's that on the envelope?"

"Whaddyamean?" Tank answered.

"Turn it over," Junior instructed.

Tank obeyed and stared hard at handwriting that seemed to have been scribbled in haste. He then began to read the words: "This envelope contains a letter from my employer, Miss Harriett Keyser. Open this envelope only in the presence of an attorney and a witness. Failure to open this document in the described manner may seriously jeopardize the contents herein." It was signed, "Ralston Bazzle, chauffeur and friend to Miss Harriet Keyser."

"What's 'Jeperdize' mean?" Munch asked.

"Idiot, jeopardize means if we open it without a lawyer and a witness the contents inside the envelope might be worthless or something like that," Junior trailed off.

"I say we open it right now. It could be a map, buried treasure, that sorta' thing," Munch said.

"No, we can't do that. This must be important stuff and we need to think about this," MV cautioned. "I say we keep the bag and letter here until we can talk with someone about what we should do. Besides, we have no right to the bag, it's not ours." A loud bang on the door of the Lattice Works startled us.

"What are you kids doing in there?" my dad demanded, pushing the door open. Tank hid the bag behind him as Dad adjusted his eyes from sunshine radiating off white and melting snow to the shadows within the Lattice Works. I was wrong in my calculations; Dad was not coming home late tonight—he was already here.

"Not doin' anything, Dad! We're just havin' a meetin' of the Maple Avenue Gang, that's all," I replied cheerfully, wondering how I had misjudged his travel time. Munch, Tank, Jazz Man, Junior, MV and Randy all hoisted smiles similar to mine and they each executed little waves at Bill Ryan.

Dad grinned and said, "Oh, big conference, huh? Ok, but you'd better conclude your business if you want to have supper on time. And don't mess with the lawnmower or any of the paint down here," Dad said and then stopped. I saw his eyes go to the floor.

"Charlie, why is my mallet here? Did you get that from the garage?"

I froze. My dad was obsessive about his tools. I could feel the switching that would be applied to my behind.

MV stepped in. "Daddy, we needed a mallet and a wrench and, uh, this here pair of pliers to work on a lock. Well, not really a lock, but the latch on the lattice door. It was loose. Charlie got the mallet and the slip-wrench and fixed it. Didn't need the pliers, as it turned out. All fixed now, Charlie was just about to take 'em all back to the garage."

I noticed Munch, Tank, Jazz Man, Junior, and Randy were nodding affirmatively and that MV's fingers were crossed behind her back.

"Yep, that's right, Dad. Gonna' take 'em back right now," I said, making a show of reaching for the tools, finally doing my part in the cover-up.

"Just give them to me. You know not to mess with my tools. Next time, ask me first," Dad said with a wink.

"Yes, sir!" I said, relieved and happy. Dad closed the lattice door and was gone. The mallet, slip-wrench and pliers were firmly in Dad's massive hands, headed for their proper place in Bill Ryan's coveted array of tools.

"Well, so much for the Ryan kids not lying to their parents," Randy chortled.

"Did not lie, just a fib, my fingers were crossed. We were

working on a lock. Just a little fib, but a grain of truth, that's different," MV said, stomping her foot.

"I guess we don't have to look for a lawyer, we got one right here," Tank said, grinning at MV.

− 16 −

I blew the whistle three times, confident my lips would not freeze even though the temperature had begun to lower and a heavy snow was predicted. We waited at the perimeter of the Pullman graveyard. Within minutes, Sonny Longsten appeared from around the nearest Pullman car. He carried two buckets, each full of water, balancing them as he maneuvered the snow-covered ground that separated us.

"Well, well, if it ain't the Maple Avenue gang," he said, grinning at us as we stood motionless.

"Yep, all of us, and we got business," I replied.

"Business?"

"Yep, need to hire a lawyer."

"Lawyer?"

MV took over. "Your friend, Mr. Wenning. Didn't he tell Mom and us he was a lawyer?"

"Yeah, he might have mentioned it, but he hasn't practiced law in years."

"See this satchel?" MV said, hoisting the bag above her head. "Found it on one of the Pullman cars. It's got papers inside that say they have to be witnessed by a lawyer," MV said.

"And a second witness," Junior instructed.

"No kidding. Well, aren't you folks a surprise," Sonny said, setting the buckets of water on the ground. "Give it to me," he said, pulling off gloves, extending a hand, reaching toward MV, obviously asking to see the satchel.

MV walked toward Sonny, bag in hand, ready to give it to Sonny.

"Stop! We need the lawyer first," Junior sputtered, shaking his head at MV. MV did stop and looked at me for guidance. I stood mute, not knowing what to do.

Sonny laughed a laugh I had a hard time interpreting. The laugh seemed harsh.

"Give me the papers, then we can decide if we should see Josh," he demanded.

"No, I think Junior's right. The instructions here are that an attorney has to see 'em first," MV said, rethinking the situation. Munch, Randy, Tank, Jazz Man and I offered our support to Junior and MV's position, nodding in the affirmative. Sonny just stared at us and then he relented.

"Okay, if that's the way it has to be, follow me," he said, lifting the buckets of water and turning on his heel, a frown on his face.

We quickly ran to catch up with Sonny who was moving rapidly down a path between two rows of cars as the snow began.

"Is he angry?" I whispered to MV.

"Don't know, he acted funny," MV said, clutching the bag as we half-walked, half-ran behind Sonny's long gait.

"Yeah, he's mad about something, all right," Munch panted as the cold, snow, and wind became more intense. "I think he got mad because we'll only talk with the lawyer. We don't need him."

"We do need him," I shot back, "He's the witness."

"Quit gabbing. He's gonna' hear you," Randy warned.

"Oh! Scares me a lot! You're just a big chicken!" Tank said, looking at Randy and laughing out loud.

"Tank, just shut your mouth," MV hissed.

Tank continued to laugh as he strode along, a full head taller than the rest of us. We turned the corner on one row of cars and advanced to yet another corridor of Pullman cars, this row supplying a blissful break from the wind.

The fifteen-minute walk led us deeper into the graveyard than we had ever gone, and I realized as the snow quickly erased our tracks we might have trouble finding our way out without Sonny's help. I hoped Junior was memorizing the path and that Sonny was not all that angry.

Sonny finally stopped, placing the water buckets on the snow.

"You are in my territory now and you have to do what I say. You'll need help to get out of here in this weather. I walked a serpentine path so as to purposefully confuse you. Don't even try to remember where this car is and don't ever bring anyone here," Sonny said, his eyes narrowing as he stared intently at each of us. We all nodded as the snow enveloped us and the cold permeated our clothing.

The windows of the car Sonny had led us to were covered in grime and the exterior looked as though this particular Pullman had been setting in disrepair long before I was born.

Satisfied he had made his point that we were in a restricted area, Sonny climbed the steps to the rear of the car and inserted a key. He pushed the door open and beckoned to us. We filed aboard, entering the car with great trepidation, expecting more spiders, rats or even raccoons.

"Holy cow," I heard Tank exclaim as he entered the car at the head of our pack, ducking down. Additional exclamation was heard from each of our gang as we invaded the Pullman. Bringing up the rear, I finally got a glimpse of what the commotion was all about.

The interior of the car was a shock to each of us; I took in the sight of heavy, rich fabric, beveled glass, dark and highly polished wood. There were decorative and intricate patterns of flowers, fruit and animals on the pristine mahogany. I did not know I was looking at "Marguetry"—the art of forming intricate patterns by the insertion of pieces of wood into a veneer, a technique chosen by George Pullman himself. The result was simply stunning.

We walked by sleeping rooms that were plush, our eyes

bulging as we took in the detail of the elaborate coach. Wide-eyed, we eventually came to the car's dining area where we saw Josh Wenning conversing with Sonny. Josh stood behind a polished bar that reflected off the crystal glasses on shelving behind him. My eyes widened even more as I spotted a fully lit Christmas tree and candy canes. At the same time, I realized what had caused Sonny to alter his tone with us; Sonny was risking his neck by bringing us aboard. He had been seriously agitated when we insisted upon being taken to see our lawyer, but he had not been nearly as angry as Josh was at this moment.

"Are you nuts? You can't bring anybody in here, let alone these kids!" Josh hissed at Sonny in a high-pitched squeal.

"Well, I guess I've already done that, so just settle down and I'll explain everything."

"No need to explain—get out! Get your stuff and get out. I gave you a place to stay, a roof over your head, food and water, and all I asked was discretion—that you not tell anyone about the Pullman Hilton, let alone bring anyone here. Get out before I do something that I'll regret. Get your butt out of here. That goes for all of you!" Josh shouted, moving his hardened gaze to us, slamming a hammy fist on the bar.

"No, wait! You can't do that, sir," I heard someone say. I looked behind me and there was MV holding the satchel high. She was, I thought, as crazy as Sonny, challenging the giant behind the bar.

I assumed at that point that we were all dead.

"What's that?" Josh asked, seeing fine leather.

"We found it in one of the Pullman cars—hidden behind a panel," Junior interjected. "You better take a look, seein' as how you're a lawyer."

"What's he talking about?" Josh demanded, looking at Sonny.

"Kids say there are papers in the satchel that need to be taken to an attorney. You're an attorney, they want to retain you," Sonny said.

"That does it! Out! Out, everybody! I won't stand to be ridiculed! Get out of my home, go!" Josh exploded.

Out of nowhere we were aware of a tall black man in our midst, dressed to the nines. He put his finger to his lips, looked at Josh and said, "Shhhhhh."

"Arthur?" Josh said.

"Might as well hear them out, don't you think? You're not the only lawyer in the room, you know."

"I know, I know," Josh said, emitting a long sigh. His large shoulders sagged and he turned to us and said, "This is Mr. Arthur Boreman—Arthur Boreman, Esquire. He worked as a Pullman porter for ten years on the B&O Blue Line and earned enough money to go back to school—law school—at Howard University. Got his law degree and tried to get a practice going but there's not much business for black lawyers. So—," Josh said, trailing off.

"So I came back to the B&O, back to the Blue Line, picked up where I left off, as a porter, same as lots of porters who got college degrees. Never did practice much, but I'd like to see if I could help out here," Arthur said, winking at MV.

"No kidding?" Sonny responded. "You didn't tell me that," Sonny said, looking at Josh, "Arthur's really a lawyer?"

"Exactly, no kidding," Arthur said, cocking his head to one side as Josh nodded affirmatively.

"Are you two lawyers just talk? Can we get down to business here?" Tank interjected, his chin raised in defiance as he glanced from Josh to Arthur and back.

"Smart aleck kid, huh? Well, tell you what, Arthur may like what he's hearing but not me. Sorry, Arthur, but this is not good," Josh said, turning toward the Pullman porter, frowning. "These kids are going to bring us down. So, you represent them, Arthur, and God bless. Tell you what, though, this means we're going to lose the Hilton," Josh said, his high voice trembling.

Arthur's face darkened and he turned away, hurt and disappointed. The air was filled with tension and my sister stepped forth.

"Mr. Wenning," she began, "we apologize for bursting through the door and all that. We didn't mean to, uh, invade your territory. Fact is, this is something we don't completely understand but we do know it's a mystery that needs to be solved. We don't know many attorneys, well, make that we don't know any attorneys, but we think we mighty sure need one. I guess it's not related in any way, but my mom sure liked you, trusted you, and I think you're the kind of hobo, uh, lawyer, that can make a real difference in unraveling this thing we've gotten into."

Silence.

We waited in trepidation as Josh looked away, washing his eyes over the interior of the Pullman car, taking in the home he obviously loved. He shook his head, ran his fingers through his hair, and looked directly at MV.

"Tell you what, little lady, it's Christmas and I think it'd be a good thing if I tried to do a good deed. Give me the satchel, let's see what we have."

Sonny exhaled and relaxed. Arthur smiled. MV had calmed the Beast.

– 17 –

Josh and Arthur sat at one of the tables in the dining area of the car. Josh placed the satchel in front of Arthur and opened it. He drew out the partially damaged, sealed envelope and read the instructions from Ralston Bazzle that had brought us to Josh Wenning and Arthur Boreman, our newly-found attorneys.

Josh asked Sonny to fetch him a pencil from a cabinet behind the bar and some slightly discolored stationery he had found months ago in one of the Pullman cars.

Josh wrote and read at the same time; "This is to acknowledge that I, Josh Wenning, attorney-at-law—uh, Arthur, do you want me to add your name?" he asked.

Arthur chuckled and said, "No, better not, I'd hate to have to appear in court."

"Okay," Josh continued, "I, Josh Wenning, attorney-at-law, have in my possession an envelope with a message written on it, dated April 1, 1931. One Ralston Bazzle, chauffeur and friend to Miss Harriet Keyser, has signed a message on the envelope. Mr. Bazzle instructs the finder of said envelope to open it only in the presence of an attorney and a witness. I, Josh Wenning, am the attorney that the finder of said envelope..."

Josh paused and looked at the Maple Avenue Gang.

"Who's the finder?" he asked.

"That'd be me," Tank replied.

"No way," Junior objected. "MV found the bag and letter."

The Maple Avenue Gang, save for Tank, all concurred. Tank just smiled and looked at MV. "Guess ya' got me on that one, Junior. MV did find it. Course I pulled it out of the hole it was in."

"Alright, so MV found it," Arthur interjected, softly. "Tell us again, what does MV stand for, little lady," Arthur asked, his face spreading into a wide smile that transformed him into a gentle giant.

"She's Mary Virginia," I piped up. "She found the bag and she made sure we kept it even when the man with the scar tried to take it," I offered.

"Man with a scar?" Arthur said, "I think I've seen him around here."

"Yep, that's the bum that stole money from us earlier and then tried to steal the bag," I said. "Randy there, or somebody, hit him with a brick, I think it might have broken some of his ribs," I offered, nodding at Randy, who smiled with satisfaction, along with Arthur.

Josh looked at Sonny with a frown that said they would have to add Scarface to a growing number of problems.

"Okay," Josh said, and resumed writing and reading his words as he proceeded to put pencil to paper; "I, Josh Wenning, am the attorney that the finder, Mary Virginia,— Josh paused. 'Ryan,' isn't it?"

"Yes, sir," MV nodded.

"Mary Virginia Ryan, has chosen to oversee the opening of the envelope on which Mr. Bazzle's instructions are written. The witness that the message instructs must be present to observe the opening of said envelope is—Sonny Longsten?"

"Okay," Sonny agreed.

Josh paused again. "What's the real name? Your parents surely didn't name you Sonny, did they?"

Sonny looked a bit embarrassed, and then said, "Winthrop. Winthrop Longsten the Third."

The Maple Avenue Gang was duly impressed. None of us, with the possible exception of Junior, had ever encountered a "Third" in our acquaintances.

"Okay, thanks, interesting," Josh grinned, looking at Sonny. "To observe the opening of said envelope is Winthrop Longsten the Third," Josh said.

I saw, looking over Josh's shoulder, that he actually wrote "Winthrop Longsten III." I thought then that Sonny must come from royalty or something, since numbers like that were always attached to the names of English and French kings.

Josh wrote his and Sonny's name at the bottom of the page. He signed after his name and Winthrop signed after his. He then added MV's name, saying, "We probably ought to also have the finder sign."

We all looked at Junior who nodded that MV should sign.

Once that was done, Josh reached for the letter itself and held it aloft. "Seems to me this is a special day. Long time since I had a client, MV," he smiled at my sister. She smiled back. The Maple Avenue Gang was having a special moment.

"Here goes. Sonny, watch closely," Josh said to his witness.

Josh carefully opened the envelope and removed the contents. He showed us two sheets of paper, both slightly soiled, with a ragged edge on the right side of each sheet. Josh spread them on the table at which he and Sonny sat, surrounded by our gang.

He read:

"I am Harriet Keyser of 5313 Mozelle Street, Paddy Town, West Virginia. I am of sound mind and body on this first day of April 1931. This letter is in the custody of my trusted chauffeur, and friend, Ralston Bazzle, and is to be delivered, at the time of my death, by him, or anyone who comes in possession of this document, to Attorney John I. Robertson at Mr. Robertson's law offices adjacent to the Mineral County Courthouse."

"I believe the will Attorney Robertson probated upon my death, unbeknownst to him, is false; specifically, it is false if it conveys property I own known as the 'Pullman Yards' to RJ Higgins. This property, my legitimate will states, is to be given at the time of my death, to the Grace Methodist Church of Paddy Town for specific use by the church as land on which is to be built a home for the elderly. I believe that Higgins duped me into signing a false document while I was under the influence of doctor-ordered medicines. The false document, I am convinced, was written by Higgins and conveyed my Pullman property to him rather than the church.

"Because of that belief, I have placed my legitimate will in a secure place known only to me; I ask that the holder of this letter secure my sealed will and take it to Attorney Robertson who is hereby instructed by me to take the steps necessary to right the wrong that has been committed. You will find the will in the…"

And here the page of stationery had deteriorated, the remaining sentences washed away by either water or heat that had invaded the Pullman car hiding place and subsequently the satchel and letter.

Josh read the letter again, shaking his head when the sentence ended without revealing the location of the will. He looked at the Maple Avenue Gang and said, "Well, what do you think?"

MV, surprising me as always, replied without hesitation, while the rest of us just stood there, not knowing what to say.

"We have to take the bag and letter to attorney John I. Robertson, at his building near the courthouse, isn't that what Miss Keyser said we should do?" MV asked. Josh smiled. He had come to really like this perky, precocious little girl.

"Exactly, MV," Arthur said in a deep and cultured voice. "Maybe Robertson will have some idea where Harriet Keyser hid her will. Certainly he will know how to proceed. Problem is, who will deliver the satchel and envelope? Sonny and Josh are hardly dressed to do that. They're vagrants as far as people in authority are concerned and they'll be treated as such. It's not likely they'd be welcome at some elegant law office."

"I'll go, not a problem," a deep voice said.

We all looked at Tank, whose hand was out, asking for the bag.

"Forget it, Tank," Junior said. "We need Josh to go. We've hired him as our attorney, uh, along with you, sir," Tank said, looking at Arthur.

"Just Josh. Josh is your attorney, he just doesn't dress like one," Arthur smiled, handsomely turned out in his beautiful porter's uniform.

"He needs a suit, doesn't he? A suit and tie like Arthur wears, or, better yet, a suit and tie like Daddy wears on Sunday to go to church," MV said. MV always said "Daddy" when referring to Dad. It was a girl thing.

"Exactly, Josh needs a suit," Arthur said, adjusting his tie, smoothing down his luxurious jacket, resplendently sartorial.

"Yeah, well, when you find a suit that'll fit old Josh here, just let me know," Josh growled at Arthur, who smiled broadly in return, leaning back, placing both hands behind his head, saying nothing.

"Daddy's suit might fit," MV said.

"Yeah," I said, "If Daddy's suit were two sizes larger."

"I think Josh could get into the jacket—couldn't button it—but he could leave the jacket open, and he could wear the pants he has on. Daddy's tie would work," MV said.

"And how do we get that suit jacket and tie?" I asked, amazed that my sister was cooking up some kind of ridiculous plot.

"We just go to Daddy's closet and borrow his jacket and one of his ties."

"Don't think he'll notice? He has two suits, when one's missing he'll notice, for sure," I said.

"Not if we borrow it before Friday. He won't even think about church 'till Friday," MV said.

"What about you, Tank, do you have a suit Josh could wear?" Munch asked, giggling, referencing Tank's enormous height and breadth.

"I wouldn't need a suit, I'd just force my way in," Tank said, exhibiting his military bravado; all things pertaining to force were pure pleasure for Tank.

"Forget it," MV said. "Tank's big, but he's not as big as Daddy; at least not yet."

— 18 —

RJ Higgins sat in his study on Carskadon Hill and looked out over Paddy Town. He nursed his Christmas toddy—whiskey that he had regularly accessed throughout the Depression from contacts that always had hooch. He turned his gaze from north to south, east to west, eyeing his properties.

The setting sun cast a shimmering light across RJ's craggy face. He shifted his spectacles under a mass of bushy eyebrows and considered his next move. His giant schnauzer Briggs nuzzled his feet as RJ re-read the city council order that gave him full permission to raze the acres he owned in North Paddy Town, clearing out the old Pullman cars there, and installing a waste disposal site.

The Pullman graveyard became his when RJ had become the beneficiary of Harriet Keyser's will. Miss Keyser grew up on farmland owning most of the area that became North Paddy Town. When she died the parcels encompassing the Pullman graveyard became RJ's. Seems Miss Keyser gave it to RJ in a will that was updated just two days before she passed on.

RJ smiled to himself and swallowed the whiskey that burned his throat as he remembered Miss Keyser's Last Will & Testament. He had seen her original will while assisting her in retrieving real estate documents from her safe deposit box. RJ had kept Miss Keyser busy reading an arcane lease she was renewing for Boggs Lumber out New Creek way while he laboriously copied parts of her typewritten will in longhand. He did not need to copy the boilerplate sections, he knew those by heart.

The original will had left the money in her bank account and her home on Mozelle Street to a niece in Westernport, Maryland. Her property on Argyle Street was given to the city for use as a playground and the land near the college was bequeathed to Catamount Tech. A considerable sum was left to the Mineral County Library that Miss Keyser frequented on almost a daily basis. Her most extensive holding, the Pullman yard, was the last gift noted.

Back in his office, RJ typed a bogus will. He did not really change much of the original document, but he altered the last bequest. Miss Keyser had given her Pullman yard real estate to the Grace Methodist Church, with the proviso the church build a home for the elderly on the property. Yes—RJ had changed that. He made himself, rather than the church, the recipient of the Pullman yard.

He remembered it as though it were yesterday. He grunted in satisfaction as he harkened back to the moment; he had handed Miss Keyser the last page of the bogus document he had prepared as she lay ill, her mind clouded by painkillers. RJ had told Miss Keyser the document was minor paperwork required by the city before fencing could be placed around one of her properties.

"What's this, RJ?" she had asked, her hand shaking as she adjusted the wire spectacles that balanced on her nose.

RJ's eyes narrowed as he leaned in toward Miss Keyser's hospital bed. "Papers that'll let me take care of that property of yours over toward Argyle Street," he said. "You remember—the city wants a fence around it because we've moved dirt out of there to use for fill on that lot out toward the college. The city fathers are all in turmoil because of the Argyle excavation. I think they're afraid kids might fall in it. Probably a good idea, saves us from any liability," RJ had lied.

Miss Keyser searched her memory but could not remember any such request by the city. But she was tired—very, very tired. She sighed, took the pen RJ offered and signed the paper.

"I'll need to put this in your safe deposit box, down to the Farmers and Merchants Bank," RJ had said, asking for the key to the box.

"Over in the dresser, top right drawer, RJ, don't lose it," Miss Keyser had replied, hovering just above consciousness.

It had all been nicely tied up. Except for one thing. A thing RJ worried about from time to time these seven years later.

He grunted and felt a tightening in his chest as he thought back to the day he had swung through the doors at the Farmers and Merchants Bank, briefcase in hand, the key from the dresser drawer in the briefcase side pocket—safe and sound.

Two weeks had passed since the hospital visit and Miss Keyser had returned home. She had called RJ's secretary, Mary Strothers, and asked that RJ return her safe deposit box key. RJ told Miss Strothers to return the call and let Miss Keyser know he'd drop off the key that very afternoon—and that he looked forward to seeing Miss Keyser with some pink in her cheeks and on the road to recovery.

Yes, he'd do that this very afternoon for sure, but not before a visit to the bank to personally place the key in the long metal container, retrieve the will, and replace it with the bogus document. RJ waived at Bill Temple, the bank president, as he moved toward the lead teller, Elsie Sheetz. He explained to Elsie he had papers of Miss Keyser and the key to her box— she had entrusted him to place the documents in safe keeping.

"How is she doing, RJ? We all love Miss Keyser—she's done so much for this town," Elsie said, as she unlocked the vault and opened the metal door that contained the bank's rows of lock boxes.

"She's frail, Elsie, frail. But she is Miss Keyser and she's home now. Can't tell, she might outlive us all," RJ said, waiting for Elsie to leave the room.

"I swan, RJ, you tell Miss Keyser we're all pulling for her," Elsie said, heading for the door.

"Will do, Elsie, will do," RJ said shutting the door. RJ waited a few moments, glanced at the clock on the wall, and opened his briefcase. He pulled the key from the side compartment of the case and inserted it in the lockbox. He grunted with anticipation as his hands searched for the will, small beads of perspiration forming.

A frown formed on RJ's face—there was a problem. He could not find the document. The metal container held jewelry and personal letters, but that was all. He searched the box several times, finally emptying the contents on the metal desk where he sat, refusing to believe the will was not there.

Muttering obscenities beneath his breath, accepting reality, he returned the jewelry and letters to the box. He drummed his fingers on the desk and thought. Then, he placed the fake will on top of the other contents, closed the box, locked it, and shoved it back in its resting place. He composed himself and walked from the bank, making certain to smile at Bill Temple and Elsie and engage in some small talk. He refrained from slamming the bank door behind him as his feet turned south on Main Street.

In the aftermath of the flawed bank plan RJ fabricated many reasons to visit Miss Keyser's house to search for the real will, even as she lay dying in her second-floor bedroom.

RJ's massive eyebrows narrowed and he poured more whiskey as he thought back on it all. He pushed deep into his chair and reviewed, for what seemed like the millionth time, a chauffeur, a chase, a mangled body and, finally, a missing satchel.

"Where was the satchel? Did it still exist? Was the will in the bag?" He had thought of everything. "What was he missing?"

He shook his head, reached down and petted the huge black dog on the floor. Briggs rolled over and RJ settled back, trying to let the whiskey do its job. His gaze drifted across Paddy Town and the State Road Garage where he had waited that stormy night. The whiskey warmed his innards and he relaxed, shifting his beady eyes from the State Road Garage to the Pullman yard. His body tensed as his gaze centered on a royal blue Pullman car.

RJ sat up with a start, inadvertently kicking his dog. "My God, Briggs" he said aloud, "how could I have missed it all these years? He hid the satchel in one of the Pullman cars!"

— 19 —

Our parents' bedroom was at the top of the stairs. MV's bedroom was to the left, mine to the right of our parents' room. My bedroom contained the door that led to the attic. The plan was to "borrow" Dad's prized Style Mart suit—actually just the coat because there was no way the slacks were going to fit Josh—and a tie from the armoire in their bedroom, and then quickly run to my room and up the stairs to stash the coat and tie in the attic.

We climbed to the second floor when we heard Mom in the kitchen, raising her ironing board, preparing to go to work on the week's ironing, dialing in "Stella Dallas" on the Philco radio that sat on a shelf in the pantry. I pulled on the door of the armoire and the big wooden repository of Mom and Dad's best clothes refused to budge.

"What's wrong?" MV whispered.

"Dang thing's stuck," I whispered back, "I've gotta' pull real hard."

"Don't cuss. Be quiet, be careful," MV said.

I yanked as hard as I could. The armoire tilted forward, about to topple on us. I pushed back with gusto and MV joined me. We both uttered sounds of alarm and gave one last shove that sent the big wooden closet back against the wall with a loud thud, causing the door of the chest to spring open.

"Charlie? Mary Virginia?" Mom yelled from the kitchen. "Are you two all right?" she asked, walking from the kitchen to the living room and the bottom of the steps, ignoring Stella Dallas.

"We're okay, Mom!" I shouted. "I dropped my, uh, Erector set on the floor, we're building a, uh, a Ferris wheel."

"Well, alright, sure that's all?"

"Yes, Momma', that's all; we're fine," MV assured Mom.

"Alright, lunch soon, we're having Sloppy Joes, you'll be glad to know," Mom said, amusement in her voice; she knew I began to salivate at the mere mention of the barbecue sandwich we called a "Sloppy Joe". I almost forgot about the task at hand until MV pulled my dad's suit off the rack, taking the jacket from the hanger, giving it to me.

"Pick out a tie," she said.

"What color?" I asked.

"I don't think it matters, but something a lawyer would wear."

I reached for the most colorful, loudest tie I could see, assuming a lawyer would want to be noticed.

"Better get the longest one, too, so's it'll go around a big, big neck."

I then grabbed the longest tie I could find, not quite as colorful as the first tie I had chosen, but it did feature a bright red swirl on a magenta background. Loud. It would work for a lawyer.

We carefully closed the armoire and hustled to my room where we opened the door to the attic and climbed the stairs. Shoving aside old copies of *Ripley's Believe It Or Not* from a dusty trunk top, we cleaned the surface and laid the jacket and tie flat. We placed a blanket over them, shielding the clothing from sight.

We looked at one another and I asked the question: "How do we get the jacket and tie out of the attic?"

"We'll wait 'till Daddy and Mom are out of the house," MV replied.

"Or Canasta night," I said, referring to the Canasta games that took place between Mom and Dad and our neighbors, Calvin and Eleanor McCoole. This night of cards would be special, with a Christmas cake and ice cream. Their attention would be glued to the seasonal fest.

"Great idea," MV said. "Canasta night. That'll work."

— 20 —

The next evening MV and I waited until the Canasta game got very tense and then crept to the second floor and entrance to the attic. We climbed the stairs, retrieved Dad's coat and tie and folded them gently into a shopping bag from McCoole's Men's Store.

We eased down the steps with our bag and into the living room and on to the kitchen where we crept out the back door and into the cold. We ran to the side of the house, depositing the bag and its contents in our Lattice Works headquarters under the front porch. We then beat a hasty, shivering retreat to the kitchen and waited for the card players to call for holiday refreshments whereupon we helped ourselves to hefty bowls of ice cream.

Next morning, two days before Christmas, we headed for the Pullman yard. Munch, Tank, Jazz Man, Junior, and Randy pummeled us with questions about the shopping bag we were carrying. We filled them in on its contents, walking as fast as we could.

I blew my whistle as we entered the yard. We waited. Fifteen minutes went by. Finally, Sonny and Josh appeared from around one of the Pullman cars, cautiously checking for intruders other than ourselves.

Once again, we were led on the serpentine route through the snow back to the Pullman Hilton. It was easy to see we were still not to be trusted with the exact location of the car as Sonny walked behind us using a shovel to obliterate our tracks. Once in the Pullman, Josh wrestled his way into Dad's coat and, surprisingly enough, it didn't look too bad. He even had on a shined pair of dress shoes.

Josh smiled as he looked into the mirror behind the bar in the club car section. He said nothing, whistling to himself as he walked from the bar area, down the aisle of the car, and entered his stateroom. When he emerged he was wearing a white dress shirt and Dad's tie and jacket. He walked with pride back to where we were gathered, staring at him. He looked down at his feet.

"Never thought I'd use these size sixteen wing tips again or this dress shirt, but I'm glad I saved 'em. They don't look dated, do they?" he asked.

"Shoes look like the ones Dad wears to church on Sunday," I said. "Just not quite the same size, though." Actually, the shoes on Josh's feet looked like boats. But then again, I thought, Josh himself looked as big as pictures I had seen of ocean liners.

All in all, we agreed that Josh was now sartorially qualified to visit the offices of John I. Robertson, down by the courthouse. It also was agreed that the next morning, a Wednesday, would be the day Josh would sally forth, entering the high falutin' law offices. MV and I sat admiring Josh's large shoes when a baritone voice boomed through the car.

Out of nowhere, Arthur was standing by the bar, a glass of orange juice in his hand.

"You know," he said, "I think MV and Charlie should go with you, Josh."

"Why? What good would that do?" I asked, wondering from where Arthur had appeared.

"Well," Arthur began, "it would give Josh an additional presence. An attorney with two young charges, hard to turn down, hard to turn away, a question in everyone's mind; what's the story? Giant lawyer, little girl and boy." Arthur winked at MV and continued. "Besides that, MV found the satchel, she can testify in person, backing up her signed document. I think they should go, just to make sure John I. Robertson will talk with you, Josh."

We understood. Arthur made sense. A bit of mystery and a recounting of the "find" by the girl that made the discovery. I had little doubt MV could assist Josh in any legal discussion or dispute that might arise, and I looked forward to witnessing the party. First, however, Arthur counseled that Josh needed to make certain his understanding of current real estate law was the same as when he last practiced. Josh agreed, walked to the bar and gave Arthur a giant hug, calling Arthur his co-counsel, glancing at Sonny, informing him he was his newly found legal assistant. "Got a real law firm here! Wenning, Boreman and Longsten, Attorneys-at-Law!" Josh guffawed, voice high.

Arthur grinned and immediately took control, telling Josh he needed to access a copy of the State Code, something all lawyers had in their offices, to make certain any case he presented was up-to-date with the law. Josh readily agreed and suggested a library might have a copy of the State Code.

"Mineral County Library, under the yellow schoolhouse," I said.

"That's where you go for all your reading?" Josh asked.

"Yeah, Charlie knows it like the back of his hand," MV said.

"Okay, thing is, can you find it without raising suspicion?" Josh asked.

"I've got a library card," I boasted.

"Not that, it's just that a ten-year-old kid doesn't ask for a copy of the State Code. Questions are certain to be asked," Josh frowned.

"Tell ya' what," Tank said, "Charlie can just go in, look around, and find the book. He's in there all the time, knows his way around. He can grab the book and hide it under his shirt, just walk out."

"Well, depends upon the size of the book," I said, worried, and offered another idea.

"There's a window back of the stacks. I can open the window and pass the book to Tank," I said.

"Charlie," MV said, "that would be stealing."

"No, not if I got the book back as soon as our lawyers read it. I've got a library card, it's not a stealin' thing," I said, jaw jutted out.

"Seems to me Charlie is correct," Josh said. "We can borrow the book and return it within 24 hours. The library card gives us some leeway."

We all looked at Arthur. He looked around at all the things in the Pullman car that Josh had "borrowed," gave a faint smile, and nodded assent.

Tank and I were delighted.

— 21 —

RJ Higgins opened the back door to his office on Carskadon Hill. He threw off his overcoat, ignoring the wet snow that clung to the heavy garment. He beckoned the man with the large scar on his face to come inside out of the cold. The thin man hurried through the door and into the foyer, hesitating slightly when he saw RJ's dog, Briggs. The black giant schnauzer, large but gentle in nature, growled at Scarface, knowing what was coming. Scarface did not disappoint, swiftly kicking at the dog's ribs, not once but twice. The dog barked as the first thrust struck only a glancing blow and then howled as Scarface connected with his second attempt. The schnauzer backed away, growling a low guttural sound, turned, and ran to the interior of the large house.

RJ stepped back to the foyer and yelled at Scarface, "Rem! Leave him alone! Touch him again and I'll see that your ribs get busted!" RJ said, glancing toward the whimpering, cowering dog.

"You know I can't stand a filthy dog. I've got a scar right here on my face from a lousy Pit Bull that came after me when I was three. It's not just that big old hairy pony of yours—I hate all dogs! Keep your flea infested animal away from me," Scarface hissed, his fingers tracing the scar on his face.

"Get in here, now!" RJ instructed, pointing to his office. Scarface smirked and walked into a wood-paneled sanctuary with deep leather chairs and an open cabinet lined with liquor bottles. Scarface moved quickly to the bar, a route he had traveled many times before when RJ needed his assistance.

"Try the rye, Rem, W.H. McBrayer's —93 proof—you'll like it," RJ said, trying to control his anger over the attack on Briggs, preparing Scarface to accept his assignment.

"Whaddya' need this time, Higgins?" Rembrandt Simmons said, pouring a double shot of rye whiskey, knocking it back with one fell swoop, then pouring another.

"Easy, Rem, no need to get sloppy."

"Sloppy is sometimes a good way to be, helps with the mental attitude down to the jungle, know what I mean, Higgins?"

"Don't know why you insist on livin' in the hobo jungle, Rem, you could get a room over at the Tourist Home on Potomac Drive or even the Corwin Hotel on Main, all the money you're takin' from me."

"Wine, women, and song, as the sayin' goes, Higgins. That don't leave much for a bed under a roof; tent's good enough for me."

"Your choice. Now, let's get down to business."

Scarface poured another shot and flopped into a red leather chair in front of RJ's desk. Higgins's eyes again narrowed to slits and he began to outline the job he had for the now slightly intoxicated man who sat before him.

"I'm lookin' for a little black satchel," RJ began.

Scarface listened intently as RJ relayed his story; he was certain there was a small leather satchel hidden somewhere in the Pullman graveyard. If Scarface were to find the bag there would be a considerable reward. The assignment, like others he had given Scarface in the past, was to be of a confidential nature; RJ added that the confidentiality must not be violated in any drunken stupor in which Rem might find himself in the future.

"Big yard, needle in a haystack, it may never turn up," Scarface said, irritated at the footnote that he was obviously a drunk.

"And that's just fine if it doesn't. But I want you to comb the yard, try your best to locate the bag. If you don't, somebody else might find it—or somebody might already have it. Those bums you live with in the jungle, one of them might have found it. This is important, Rem, if you ever find it, there's a thousand dollars in it for you."

The reward money was huge, but Scarface mused to himself it would grow to an even larger sum when he had his hands on the bag. He smiled as he felt the still sensitive ribs where the brick had hit. He was drunk at the time, true enough, but not drunk enough that he had forgotten the scene; five kids, plus the two he had accosted earlier, a small satchel flying through the air; a satchel that had been hidden in the Pullman. He knew who had the bag RJ sought, and he would squeeze

Higgins for a far greater return than the thousand when he eventually handed the satchel over. All he had to do was find the seven kids. It would be good to repay them for his bruised body and ego.

Scarface hummed softly to himself as he walked down the driveway and away from Higgins' home. He did not notice Briggs standing at the large bay window in the living room of the antebellum home. The dog's shiny black coat bristled as the schnauzer's gaze fixed on the man. A low growl filled the room.

— *22* —

Paddy Town's streets had been cleared once more and I parked my bike outside the Mineral County Public Library and went over the drill again with Tank. He was to wait beside the rear window of the library and I would pass out any books I found to him. The window opened into a well that allowed light to pass into the rear stacks of the library. Tank grunted his assent and understanding, blowing into his hands to warm them. "Piece of cake, storm troopers on the move," he said, snapping a smart salute to me.

"Tank, if you were ten years older you'd have a flamethrower in your hand," I said.

Tank grinned, liking the idea. I shook my head and headed for the warmth of the library.

I walked down the steps into the underground of the Paddy Town Grade School where the Mineral County Library was housed and shoved the door open, nodding to the librarian, Miss Florence Church. She smiled and welcomed me as enthusiastic as ever that a ten-year-old boy was a regular visitor to the stacks of books that crowded the room.

I wondered how I could move through the stacks without causing Miss Church to ask for what I was searching. Then, as luck would have it, Miss Hannah, who had been my second grade teacher, back in the day, came through the door.

She greeted Miss Church and then looked at me. "Charlie," she exclaimed. "So good to see you. I am so glad you are still visiting the library even during Christmas vacation."

"Yes, ma'am, I'm reading all the time," I said, beaming that she was excited I was frequenting the library.

Miss Hannah and Miss Church engaged in lengthy conversation and I was free to begin my search for the State Code in earnest. I made my way slowly around the stacks and went to "Politics", "Biographies", and "Current Events" and found nothing. I surveyed areas that were too adult for me, checking out "Foreign Affairs" and "International Business". I was about to give up when I turned from one stack to the next, and looked up. There it was.

"Law", said the simple statement, under which there were several rows of books. I reached in my pocket and withdrew Arthur's instructions: "Look for the State Code or any volume that says Property Law or Real Estate Transactions or something resembling that," he had written.

I saw nothing that looked like the State Code. My eyes moved down toward the row of books that were at face level.

One book was obviously new. The spine carried the words I knew would bring a smile to Sonny's face and supply all that Josh would need. The title read, "State Property Law Treatise-1935 Edition."

Bingo. I did not need the State Code, I reasoned, all I needed was this one book. I grabbed the book from the shelf and walked the length of the library. At the far end of the rows of stacks was a small window that opened into a window well at the base of the grade school foundation.

I was alarmed that the window was out of my reach. I looked around for something to stand on and saw nothing. I retraced my steps, checking each row between the stacks, looking for anything on which I could perch. The last row revealed a large stool and my pulse returned to normal. I dragged the stool toward the window hoping the scraping noise could not be heard out where Miss Church and Miss Hannah were gabbing. I placed the stool at the bottom of the window and climbed to the ledge. The stool was heavy and I was out of breath. I put the book on the ledge of the window and tried the latch to see if it worked. It opened easily and the glass pane swung forward, a blast of cold air hitting me in the face. I looked for Tank's shoes, but saw only snow. "Tank!" I hissed. No reply.

I eased up onto the windowsill, undulating back and forth like a porpoise, finally squeezing through the window into the well that allowed light into the library. I reached back, grabbed the book, and placed it beside me in the well. I looked up and saw Tank's face where his shoes should be. He was on his knees, grinning down at me, his hand outstretched to receive the book. I reached as far as I could, but we could not quite connect.

Trying to extend myself to shorten the space between our two hands, I suddenly realized I had made a bad mistake; the stool tipped as I leaned forward, and it clattered sideways onto the floor. I held my breath, waiting for Miss Church to come flying down the stacks, looking for the source of what sounded to me like a cannon. I put my finger to my lips, signaling Tank to be quiet. I felt as though I might wet my pants; seconds ticked by and no one appeared. I again relaxed; and then I realized I was solidly stuck, jammed into the window frame. I shimmied back and forth, trying not to make any noise. Tank, seeing my predicament, stretched toward me, to no avail.

"Gimme the book, dang it," he whispered, his face red from the cold and his crouched effort as he peered down into the well.

"I'm stuck, what am I gonna' do?" I cried, nearing tears.

Tank squeezed himself into the window well, held his breath, and grabbed the book. I feared he himself would be stuck since his large torso was packed into the space like sardines in a can. He twisted and grunted and moved himself like a cement mixer, finally lifting himself out of the hole. I saw only his hands and feet as he placed the real estate book on the ground beside his Camelback Schwinn, the bike I secretly coveted. Craning my face upward I watched as the book disappeared, and heard the sound of Tank plopping on the bike, the springs responding to his considerable mass, and then he was gone. I could not believe Tank had abandoned me. I was trapped in my porpoise-like pose, my butt sticking out into the stacks of the Mineral County Public Library and Tank had taken off. I hoped Miss Hanna would not see my rear end jutting from the window.

Then, from within, the front of the library, I heard Tank.

"Howdy, Miss Church, Miss Hannah, Merry Christmas!" Tank said in a jovial manner.

"Why, John, how wonderful to see you here," Miss Church responded, using Tank's given name, something we seldom uttered.

"Yeah, is Charlie here?"

"Yes, he's back there. Hope you'll join him with some Christmas vacation reading, John," Miss Church said.

"Yeah, I'm gonna' try to, can't tell, I might even make a withdrawal today," Tank said, grinning, walking away from the two women and down the stacks toward my protruding behind.

Tank laughed a boisterous laugh when he saw me, assessed his options, and took charge. He grabbed both of my legs and gave a powerful tug. I popped out of the window and came crashing to the floor on top of my large friend. My nose was red and I was half covered in snow.

"Charlie, John, are you alright?" came the call from Miss Church.

"Yes, dropped a few books, I'm awfully sorry. Tank and I are putting them back, nothing to worry about, nothing damaged," I called back, as Tank pushed me off his chest.

"Pretty funny, you didn't have to pull that hard," I hissed at Tank, rubbing my behind.

"Just be glad I didn't use a crowbar," Tank said, grinning from ear to ear.

I pulled the stool back to the windowsill and reached in and closed the window, wiping the snow and wet from the windowsill with my jacket sleeve. I then hurried after Tank to the front of the library where we said goodbye to Miss Church and Miss Hannah, wishing them a happy holiday. They barely acknowledged us as we walked out; they were deep in conversation. I climbed the few steps from the library, boarded my bike and joined Tank as he sped away, book in hand.

— 23 —

MV was with Arthur in the Pullman Hilton, digging through a large box of Christmas ornaments Josh had produced from somewhere—no one dared asked exactly "where". They were waiting for Tank and me to show up, hopefully with the State Code.

"Wow! Look at this Arthur," MV said, pulling a glass angel from the box, "I can't believe someone threw this away, it's beautiful!"

"Sure is, and let's hope no one's missing it," Arthur winked, taking the angel and placing it atop the Christmas tree, beginning to add ornaments to lights.

"Yeah, guess Mr. Josh has some secrets to keep. Still, he's an awfully nice man," MV said, watching Arthur tilt the angel just so. The Pullman car was warm enough, but Arthur had donned a gray sweater to ward off any chill that might invade the premises. His suit jacket was draped across a chair.

"How come you have such a beautiful suit, Arthur?" MV asked, looking at the jacket, then squinting up at the tall, handsome black man.

"Well, we porters in charge of luxury cars were required to dress in a uniform that would be every bit as fine as the clothes our passengers would wear. They were affluent people and dressed mighty fine. My uniform is original, but I have taken some liberties—this red tie, for instance—I don't want the good Lord to miss me if he looks for me, so I replaced my black bow tie with this red necktie," he said, softly stroking the red silk tie that stood out starkly against his blue jacket.

"Hand me another, MV," Arthur said, pointing at the box of ornaments.

"Arthur?"

"Yes?"

"What does 'affluent' mean?"

"Well, it generally meant folks on this car were rich. Lots of money."

"Arthur?"

"Yes."

"Are you a ghost?"

Arthur chuckled, "You might say that, but I prefer to think of myself as a spirit—a friendly spirit," he said, smiling down at MV as she continued to dig through the treasure trove of Christmas decorations.

MV cocked her head and said, "Why are you here? Ghosts, uh, spirits, generally are around only if they can't get to Heaven." She bit her lip, wondering if she had crossed the line.

Arthur paused, his hand wrapped around a porcelain snowflake, and emitted a long sigh. "Fact is," he said, "that's a pretty accurate statement." He then told MV the story of the fateful Christmas Eve he and the small passenger for whom he was responsible died.

"It was my fault. I was supposed to be awake, make sure my passengers were safe and sound," Arthur said, his face filled with sadness.

"But, you tried to save her. And you died doing it. You didn't do anything so bad—you just fell asleep," MV said, looking at Arthur, her tears beginning to form.

"I know, child, I know. But I keep telling myself the good Lord may see it differently. I don't have a bad life here, it's interesting, just coming and going. But, one day, I'd like to meet my Lord and Savior and be welcomed home," Arthur said, leaning down to MV, smiling.

"You still like Christmas and Christmas Eve though, right?"

"Oh, yes, child, my mistake, tragic as it was, has never erased the beauty and message of the Christ child. I lost a child's life and then my own, but the life of that child born in Bethlehem will always be there, guiding us. I hope I will be guided by that light and be welcomed to a heavenly home—one day."

MV leaned toward Arthur and put her small arm across his broad shoulder. "I know that day will come, Arthur. Mom and Dad say faith is the answer to all our troubles and I know I've got faith you'll leave the Pullman Hilton some day and get to Heaven."

Arthur put his burly arms around MV, fell to his knees and hugged her, whispering in her ear, "My dear little girl, you give me great hope and much joy and I will always be here for you."

— 24 —

Christmas carols filled the air as Tank and I rode our bikes down the hill, turned left onto Armstrong Street, and headed toward the sound of Bing Crosby and Jingle Bells. The music was pumping from RJ Higgins' Merry-Go-Round and Ferris wheel. Weather permitting, every winter Higgins removed his carousel and Ferris wheel from mothballs and erected it at Armstrong and North Davis Streets to serve as the focal point for the town's winter carnival. He bragged to *The Paddy Town Daily News* that it was Higgins' gift to the community, but even in the Depression, he charged for the rides, covering his costs, and in some years made a few bucks.

The winter of '38 was frigid at times, but the cold and snow relented somewhat as we neared Christmas week and Higgins was set to do business. I glanced toward the Ferris wheel as we crossed the B&O tracks and shuddered as I spied RJ Higgins stepping from the control housing of the big wheel. The stout little man wore a black overcoat and heavy scarf and looked my way with those beady eyes. I had always feared Higgins and his wheel and now, if Harriet Keyser's fears proved real, I had even more reason to be concerned.

I was blowing my whistle as we rode into the Pullman yard. We laid our bikes in melting snow beside bicycles already deposited there by the rest of the Maple Avenue Gang. Sonny was waiting for us. This time he took us directly to the Pullman Hilton rather than try to confuse us with his serpentine path. Melting snow removed the need to cover our tracks and I was surprised how close the Pullman was to where we entered the yard. We covered the distance in less than five minutes.

Inside the car Josh, Arthur, MV, and the rest of our gang were busy adding final touches to the Christmas tree that now shone like a star in the sky. We praised the decorations as Tank tossed the book on the table in his best military fashion. "Charlie got it and I got Charlie," he grinned, explaining my embarrassing situation at the library.

"I'd still be there if Tank hadn't come to the rescue," I admitted. Josh paid no attention; he simply sat and looked at the volume Tank had placed on the table. "This is good, real good," he said, thumbing through the book. He read silently for twenty-five minutes and then turned to his legal assistant and began dictating notes.

"Well, are we okay? Did Charlie get what you need? What's the book say?" MV asked Josh, unable to control herself any longer. Before our lawyer could answer, Arthur spoke. To our knowledge, he had never read the volume Josh was addressing. But, somehow, he seemed to know the contents.

Arthur glanced at MV and said, "I think the volume in Josh's hands tells us our assumption that real estate law pertaining to the transfer of property, by way of Last Will & Testament, has been changed at least twice since 1927."

Josh nodded in the affirmative and gestured that Arthur should continue.

"The important thing is the last change, which says bequeathed property shall hold priority status in the will of the deceased and that disputes which may arise regarding the subject property are within the jurisdiction of the probate court in the county where the property is situated," Arthur concluded.

"I agree, Arthur, very impressive. And, to me, that means if there is a separate will from the one placed on file—and we can prove it in court—then the Keyser property may no longer belong to RJ Higgins," Josh said, looking around the room.

"What's next?" Munch asked.

"Well, I don't know about you, but I'm dressed for court," Josh said, his smile widening, "or, at least, for a visit to John I. Robertson's law offices. And, Sonny, my new legal assistant, is going to go with us."

"Arthur should go, too," I said.

"I can't do that," Arthur responded, a frown crossing his face. "I can't leave the Pullman yard."

"Why not?" Junior asked.

"It's a long story. I made a few mistakes a while back and I have to stay in the yard, live here in the Pullman Hilton until I work things out."

"What kind of mistakes?" Junior queried, refusing to give up, needing more information.

Josh answered, saying, "Arthur will work it out, don't worry. He's a man to be admired. I've told him time and again he has lived his life with the highest standards. I think Arthur could leave the yard and be very happy."

"Okay," Junior said, giving up.

"You go on, I'll be right here," Arthur said and somehow, was not there at all. We kids were startled and Munch blurted, "Holy cow, where did he go?"

— 25 —

Josh set out on foot with Sonny, MV and me at his side, melting snow spraying from our footsteps. Somehow Josh had "found" a leather briefcase and he carried the worn but very lawyer-looking case in his left hand. He must have been cold for he had no overcoat; nevertheless, he gave no sign of discomfort. Sonny had gone through Josh's clothing stash and wore a shirt, tie and wool Navy pea coat.

MV carried the satchel that had contained the letter from Miss Keyser. The letter now resided inside Josh's briefcase along with Josh's documentation of the opening of the satchel. MV and I were excited that we would be front row and center at the law office when the documents would be revealed to John I. Robertson. The rest of our gang remained behind as we departed, not at all pleased to have been excluded from the visit.

MV, Josh, Sonny, and I walked through the doors of Robertson and Robertson at 2:30 in the afternoon. Christmas carols played in the distance as we sashayed right up to the front desk and just stood there. The skinny receptionist looked up at the group before her and frowned at the giant man and red beard that hovered over the holiday decorations on her desk. She then glanced down at the eleven-year-old girl and ten-year-old boy, and smiled; we were being as angelic as possible. She made a show of trying to ignore Sonny but shot several glances his way that indicated she thought he was indeed handsome.

"What can I do for you two little sweethearts?" she asked, her eyes moving from the behemoth with the red beard to MV and me.

"Thank you ma'am," MV responded, smiling brightly. "My attorney and I would like to see Mr. John I. Robertson."

"Oh?" she said, looking up at Josh, whose neck was bulging from a tight collar, his stomach protruding from a suit coat two sizes too small, topped by a tie that came only to the middle of his chest. She frowned once more and then looked down at me, smiling.

"So, which one's your attorney, honey? Big one or the cute one?" she asked MV in a manner dryer than the dirt on the Lattice Works Club floor.

"This here is my brother," MV said, putting an arm on my shoulder. "That there," she continued, looking up at Josh, "is Mr. Josh Wenning, my lawyer. And the other one," she said, pointing at Sonny, "is my lawyer's legal assistant."

The receptionist looked at Josh and said, sarcasm dripping, "Wow, big firm, legal assistant and all."

"Yes, ma'am," Josh said, his voice stressed and high. "Josh Wenning, attorney-at-law, and Sonny Longsten, best dang legal assistant in Mineral County," he added with bravado.

"And just what would your business be?" the receptionist asked, looking again at MV.

"Property law, ma'am, real estate, that sort of thing," Josh answered.

"Do tell," the receptionist said, sniffing slightly, glancing up at Josh, finally smiling at Sonny, then looking down at me, moving her stare to the left, focusing once more on MV. "Well, I'll see if Mr. Robertson can see you. He's a very busy man, you know, you should have called for an appointment."

"Yes, ma'am. It's just that this is an emergency of sorts," MV replied.

The receptionist picked up her phone and rang her boss. Moments later John I. Robertson appeared. He was a short fellow with an important way about him. He was in his shirtsleeves and suspenders, glasses perched on his nose, his tummy protruding over a thick brown belt. If he had not been bald and had, instead of his chrome dome, a beard and white hair, he would indeed have been Santa Claus.

"Yes, Miss Peterson? These are the folks who wish to see me?"

"Yes, we are," piped up MV. "My attorney, his legal assistant, and my brother and I need to see you in private. If that's okay with you."

"Well, well, young lady. You have retained counsel, have you?" John I. Robertson said, frowning, leaning down, placing his hands on his knees, his face inches from MV's. Then he smiled, and there was that Santa Claus thing again. It was in his eyes. They sparkled.

"Hhhmmpp," said Josh, who had been ignored to this point.

Glancing upward, John I. asked, "And you are counsel to this young lady, sir?"

"Yes, name's Josh Wenning, attorney-at-law, and this is my legal assistant, Mr. Winthrop Longsten the Third," Josh answered in a squeaky response.

John I. Robertson stood up from his crouch, taking in without comment the bizarre group before him, and said, "Well, Josh Wenning, attorney-at-law, I assume you are licensed to practice in this state?"

Oh, wow, I froze. I didn't know our attorney needed a license. I knew Dad needed a hunting license and I understood that, but why would an attorney need a license? He wasn't going to kill anything—or at least I hoped he wasn't.

Josh, however, didn't miss a beat. "No sir, fact is I'm not sure I'm still licensed in New York State, where I used to practice, but I don't intend to enter a courtroom or practice law here— I'm just assisting these youngsters with my knowledge of law. I hope you don't mind and are not offended."

John I. looked at Josh for what seemed like an eternity, sizing him up. Finally, he nodded his head toward the hallway and said, "I always appreciate those who attempt to assist their fellow man, Mr. Wenning. Why don't you and your client, her brother, and your legal assistant come with me," and he moved toward his office.

We followed him and entered a large room filled with books, pictures, newspapers, various awards from local and state organizations and a wooden desk that was piled high with paper and legal files. In the middle of the room was a conference table that looked worn but conjured up years of legal matters that had been initiated or concluded there. The room was comfortable, with a lived-in feeling.

"Have a seat," John I. said, gesturing toward the conference table. Josh immediately plopped into a chair and placed his briefcase on the polished surface. Sonny hesitated for a moment and then chose to sit beside him. I climbed onto a chair to Sonny's right and MV did the same to Josh's left. John I. sat across from us, leaned forward and placed his elbows on the table.

"Coffee? Hot chocolate?" he asked, looking first at Josh and Sonny and then at MV and me.

"Hot chocolate would be great," I piped up. MV rolled her eyes and Josh seemed uncertain how to answer, finally saying coffee would be welcomed. Sonny shook his head.

"Miss Peterson," he called, and his receptionist appeared at the door.

"Coffee for Josh Wenning, attorney-at-law, and hot chocolate for our little friend here. Young lady, sure you won't have some hot chocolate?" John I. asked.

"No, sir, I just want to get to the matter at hand," MV said, her face serious and intent.

"Oh," John I. said, "no time to waste, huh?" and he smiled.

"Exactly, sir," MV replied.

"Cream, Mr. Wenning?" asked Miss Peterson, smiling at Sonny.

"No ma'am, just black," Josh replied, tugging at his tie.

Miss Peterson left the room in search of the designated drinks. She hesitated at the door, looked back, and smiled once more at our legal assistant as she left the room.

"Alright, Mr. Wenning, proceed," John I. said, glancing at his departing secretary, and then winking at Sonny.

Josh began to tell the tale and John I. Robertson's smile vanished when he heard the name Harriet Keyser.

His face grew stern as we relayed our discovery of the satchel and the subsequent revelations of the letter inside the bag.

— 26 —

"Let me get this straight," John I. said, "you have a letter from Harriet Keyser that says the will we probated after her death is a fake?"

"That's what it says," Josh replied, and pushed the letter across the table to John I. "My legal assistant and I have researched this and our interpretation of the updated real estate law in this state makes it clear that any inherited real estate whose testamentary conveyance is challenged reverts to probate court for determination of ownership and distribution purposes," Josh said.

John I.'s eyebrows went up. "I'm impressed, Mr. Wenning— that's a bit of arcane law that most folks don't know about. The state legislature fiddled around with the code a few years ago. How did you know about that?"

Josh looked at me and pulled the real estate volume from his case. "Charlie made a withdrawal at the county library," he said.

John I. glanced at the book and then at me and said, "Always helps to have a good researcher in a law firm." He adjusted his spectacles, picked up the letter, and read it aloud. He then read it once more, silently, to himself.

The secretary came back with the coffee and hot chocolate, placing it between Sonny and me, her face close to Sonny's as she did so. Sonny, for his part, turned beet red.

John I.'s eyes twinkled with amusement, but only for an instant as he returned to the business at hand. "This is very upsetting to me," he said. "Harriet Keyser was a very intelligent lady. If she believed RJ Higgins altered her will, there must be something to it. Trouble is, without the will, which she says she has secured in a safe place, unknown to us, we have no proof," John I. said.

"Exactly," Josh concurred. "Without the original, Higgins may never be brought to justice. He's got the upper hand."

"An upper hand that will soon be dealt, Mr. Wenning," John I. Robertson said, informing us that in the spring of the year Higgins' plans were to raze the Pullman cars on his property and break ground at the Pullman yards to begin construction of a garbage disposal site.

"What?" Josh said. "He's going to level the yard?"

"Everybody knows that," MV said. "Daddy says it'll make a mess of Maple Avenue."

"MV's right," I said, remembering hushed conversations my parents had had in the past few months after reading various articles in *The Paddy Town Daily News*.

"He'll take out all the cars first, then they'll do excavation for the incinerator that'll be used. RJ plans to take garbage from all over the tri-state area. It's awful for Paddy Town, but it'll certainly make RJ rich beyond his dreams," John I. said.

"We've got to stop him," Josh said, "the Pullman Hilton can't be destroyed."

"Pullman Hilton?" John I. asked, his eyebrows again lifting.

"Yeah," MV piped up, pointing at Josh and Sonny, "their offices and home are in the Pullman Hilton, in the yard." MV stopped abruptly as Josh's large hand covered her mouth and most of her face.

Moving to fill an awkward void, Sonny said, "Never mind. We've got to think; what interests did Miss Keyser have, where did she go? What routine did she have? Where would it be logical that she would hide her will?"

"Well," John I. began, warming to the puzzle, "she did not hold a job. Her father was quite successful and left her considerable wealth.   She gave most of it away, even before her death. Animal shelter, her church, county library, recreational parks and playgrounds; a wide array of beneficence."

"We can assume she did not secure the will in her home, correct?" Josh asked.

"I'd say so. Why would she give the chauffeur a letter that says she has placed the will in a safe place? That doesn't sound like it'd be in the house," John I. replied.

"Safe deposit box?" Sonny asked.

"Well, the will we probated was certainly in the safe deposit box but all this indicates it's a fake. Nothing else was there but personal letters and jewelry," John I. answered.

"We'll never find it. The real will, I mean," I said.

John I., Josh, Sonny, and MV looked at me in surprise, but their faces were evidence that they agreed.

We sat in silence and then MV said, "We've gotta' go, Charlie, it's almost time for supper."

"Agreed," John I. said, "let's meet here tomorrow around 2:00. That'll give me time to digest some of this and maybe we'll come up with some idea of how we can run this to ground."

We filed out of John I.'s office through an archway where Miss Peterson stood. She smiled at us and pointed upward. "Mistletoe," she said, her finger directed at a green sprig attached to the top of the archway. She then turned toward Sonny and coyly lifted her face. Sonny froze in place and we might still be there if Josh hadn't leaned down and pecked her cheek, breaking into an uproarious laugh as Miss Peterson huffed away. John I. Robertson retreated to his office, closing the door, muffling a chuckle.

MV and I departed with Josh and Sonny and walked from the courthouse up Armstrong Street, crossing the railroad tracks at Main Street, taking the alley to the Pullman yard. We said little, wondering what John I. might devise as a plan. MV and I said goodbye to our attorney and his legal assistant, retrieved our bikes from the brush where we had hidden them, climbed on, and—there was Arthur, blocking our path.

MV carried in her bike's basket the real estate volume that was to be returned to the county library. Arthur smiled, placed his hand on the basket, looked at me, and said, "Excellent work, Charlie. You and Tank may have saved the day."

"How, how do you do that?" I stammered.

"Do what?" Arthur asked, standing back, a quizzical look on his face.

"You, know, come and go like that—out of nowhere," I shot back, a bit miffed, thinking it was obvious what I meant.

"Oh, that," he said, and walked to a fallen tree at the edge of the yard and sat down on the snowy limb, motioning for us to join him. I looked at MV and then over my shoulder to see if Sonny or Josh was in sight. They were long gone and I glanced over at MV for her advice. She nodded toward Arthur and we both disembarked from our bikes and walked over to where he sat. I stood while MV sat beside him.

"Remember?" he asked me, "I told you I had made some mistakes a while back. MV knows the history so I'll tell it to you. But it's a secret between the three of us, okay?" I nodded assent and he began to tell me the story of the family aboard his last train ride, the loss of the little girl, and his death as he tried to save her. The tale seemed to be etched solidly upon Arthur's furrowed forehead.

"So, she died and you're dead?" I asked, incredulous.

"I'm afraid so," Arthur smiled.

"And, Charlie," MV said, cocking her head, "if Arthur leaves the yard he doesn't know if he'll go to Heaven or Hell."

"Yes, that's what my dream told me. Been here now about

thirty years, give or take a month or so," Arthur confirmed. He shook his head and said, "If only I could see that family once more."

I felt like a ton of bricks had fallen on me as I put it all together.

"Wait here, please!" I said, and ran for my bike. MV and Arthur looked at one another, wondering what I was doing.

I pedaled furiously, reaching our house in record time. I threw my bike to the ground and ran into the house, slamming the door behind me.

"Charlie!" Mom yelled, "How many times do I have to tell you not to slam the door?"

I ignored Mom and ran to my bedroom, throwing open the door to the attic and rushing up the stairs. There I found my stash of things I collected and saved. I shuffled through the items in the box, knowing it was there, but wondering if I had really saved it. Sure enough, there it was, near the bottom of the jumbled contents; the near-perfect photograph I had found in one of the Pullman cars in our first foray into the yard. It was the picture of a family—from some moment in time.

I put the picture in my shirt pocket, shot out of the house with Mom's chiding voice behind me as the door slammed again, and raced back to the Pullman yard, jumping from my bike as it skidded to the ground, landing in a snow bank. MV and Arthur were still sitting there, Arthur smiling at my antics.

I ran toward them, photograph in hand, and held it up for Arthur to see. "Is this them?" I asked, "Is this the family? Is that the little girl?"

Arthur's face went ashen as he looked at the photo. He took it from my hands and stared at it, his eyes wide. "Good Lord Almighty, child, this—this is the Dresser family. Hamilton Dresser, his wife, son—Lisa Lee, the daughter—I, I can't believe it. Where did you get this?"

"Found it first time we were in one of the Pullman cars. I saved it because it was in such good condition. It's yours, if you want it," I said.

"Yes, yes, I want it, thank you, thank you so much," Arthur said, looking at the picture, tears beginning to cloud his eyes. "I know now it's true, Hell awaits me."

"How do you know that?" I asked, incredulous.

"Look at Lisa Lee, she's the only one not smiling. She has a frown on her face. She wants me to know. She blames me," Arthur said.

"Wait a minute, how did the picture get into that Pullman car?" MV asked. "They, the family, they weren't in that car, they were in the Pullman Hilton," MV said.

"I don't know, someone must have taken it from their car and left it in the car where you found it—all these years—all these years," Arthur murmured, quietly placing the photograph in his shirt pocket, appearing defeated.

Well, it was all pretty overwhelming for me and I had to say something, so I said, "Why don't you bet on the odds? Josh said you were a good man, he must think you'll go to Heaven, even if Lisa Lee doesn't." Arthur smiled at me and came back to the moment.

"Yes, well, easy for Josh to think so, but it's a big step to venture out of here. I'm safe here in the yard. Out there? Well, who knows," Arthur pondered. "I've been given proof that Heaven and Hell exist. Good to know, but knowing they are for real I think about my mistakes that night and I have this terrible fear that the old Devil might be waiting for me. Lisa Lee is telling me I am right."

MV shook her head, looking up at Arthur. "Like I told you, Arthur, it has nothing to do with betting on the odds or a picture from way back then—Mom says you have to have faith," she said, frowning at me, scolding me for my brashness. "Faith that good things will result if you try to do the right thing," MV added, "and you tried to do the right thing. You tried to save that little girl."

Our conversation with Arthur ended abruptly as we heard something moving loudly through the yard. I ran to look down a corridor of nearby Pullman cars. There was Scarface, climbing aboard the rear platform of the nearest coach, entering the car. I ran back to MV and Arthur and whispered, "Scarface! He's in one of the cars!"

Arthur nodded knowingly and I felt relief, knowing that Scarface could do us no harm so long as we were with the tall black man who had befriended us. MV ran to her bike without another word and I followed. We looked back as we rode off, waving to Arthur. But Arthur was gone, his exit made much more quickly than ours.

— 27 —

Dad was searching for a certain tie. Normally he would not have cared which tie he grabbed; he wore one only on Sunday mornings when getting ready for services at the Grace Methodist Church. Yes, we were Irish but we were not Catholic. Back in County Cork in the 1800s the Protestant population was just 8%. Apparently our Ryan forefathers were part of that minority, and that's why we were in the pew at the Grace Methodist Church every Sunday.

It wasn't Sunday, but it was early Christmas Eve morning and the day of the Christmas dinner at the Masonic Lodge. Dad had crossed his fingers many times, hoping the fates that be would find him at home and not on the road the day before Christmas.

Dad had checked; he was number 9 on the "callers list"—a list of engineers to be called to run the freight trains from Paddy Town to Grafton and back. Being number 9 meant he would have plenty of time to attend the annual dinner. Those of the Catholic faith were not members of the Order of Masons; but one Catholic name, Bill Ryan, the practicing Methodist, was proud of his Masonic credentials and he was well respected in the membership of the Paddy Town Lodge.

The dinner Dad so wanted to attend was on Main Street above Murphy's Five and Dime Store where the lodge was located. The noon affair would be followed by an afternoon Christmas fair that would then lead to an evening of gaily decorated carnival booths opening near and around RJ Higgins' Ferris wheel and Carousel attractions. Dad and Mom had had their fingers crossed for months, hoping that Dad would be afforded the window of time to attend the trio of annual events, the first of which was the dinner, which demanded a suit and tie.

"Mabel, I can't find that tie with the big red swirl on it," Dad yelled down the staircase outside his and Mom's bedroom.

I was in my bedroom, listening in on the conversation. I sat on my bed beneath a pennant that I had bought at Daskin's Novelty Store. "Alcatraz" was emblazoned on the red flag. I froze when I heard Dad shout. Alcatraz Prison was where I feared I would find myself if Dad ever had any inkling what had happened to the tie. Then there was the matter of the missing coat. That would find me behind bars for sure.

"It's in the armoire," Mom shouted back.

"Well, if it's in there, I sure can't find it," Dad responded.

"Hold on, I'm coming up there," I heard Mom sigh. This happened often; Mom was the finder of things such as fingernail clippers, Dad's "Romeo" slippers, his watch chain, and various belts. Somehow he knew the location of every tool, large or small, in his workshop but the nooks and crannies of the house seemed to swallow his personal belongings.

Mom climbed the steps and headed for the armoire. I sat petrified and listened.

"Maybe it fell down to the bottom of the chest. It isn't on the rack," I heard Mom say.

"It's not in there, Mabel, I looked," Dad said with impatience.

"Well, where in the world could it be?" Mom asked, "It cannot have vanished into thin air."

"Forget about it, it'll turn up, I'll just wear another tie."

"All right, but I hate that, you had your heart set on wearing that tie. Calvin picked it out especially for you, one of the best ties McCoole's had on the rack," Mom said.

"Yeah, he gave it to me when I was initiated into the Masons. But another tie will have to do, I guess," Dad said, causing me to feel extra guilty.

Mom trundled off downstairs and I relaxed. Five minutes went by.

"Mabel," Dad shouted again. "Where's my suit jacket, the jacket to my Style Mart suit, pants are here, but the jacket's gone, where is it?"

The "Alcatraz" poster seemed to pulsate from its place on the wall, hissing, reaching for me.

Mom again climbed the stairs. This time they both spent fifteen minutes searching the armoire and the closet in their bedroom. They were puzzled and Mom was alarmed.

"Those hoboes you told me about, were they alone in the house at any time?" Dad asked Mom.

"No, I was here the whole time."

"Could they have come back? Have you found anything else missing? A suit jacket and tie don't just disappear—somebody's taken them."

"No, no, not that I know of, I'd better check, look around, see if anything else is gone," Mom said, distressed. "Should we call the police?"

"We oughta' do that if we find anything else missing; we should call them regardless if we think those hoboes over at the camp are stirring up trouble. Dang! My favorite suit and and tie!" Dad said.

"Let's think about it for a few hours, Bill—I mean, if we ask the police to help and we find out there's some other reason the jacket and tie are gone we'll, well, we'll look pretty foolish," Mom said.

"Okay, but if we don't find them we have to call Chief Dawson," Dad said, hanging his pants back in the armoire.

I slipped out of my bedroom and fled down the stairs, searching for MV. She was nowhere in sight. I opened the door to the back porch and called out for her. Tank walked around the house and said, "Lattice Works," pointing toward the porch. "Where you been?" he asked.

Not answering his question, I followed him down the walk by the house and we both stooped and entered the Lattice

Works under the front porch. MV, Randy, Junior, Jazz Man and Munch were already there. MV was filling our gang members in on the events of yesterday. I waited impatiently as she finished, saying she and I were to meet Josh, Sonny, and John I. at the Robertson law offices at 2:00 in the afternoon.

"We've got a problem," I said, looking up toward the porch floor above us. "Dad and Mom are looking for Dad's suit jacket and tie. They know they're missing and they think Josh and Sonny may have taken them," I reported.

"Uh, oh, what are they gonna' do?" Munch asked.

"They might go to the police. If they do they'll tell 'em about the two hoboes that were here and next thing we'll know the cops will be all over the hobo camp and then they'll search the Pullman cars. We'll lose our attorney if that happens," I said.

"They'll put Josh and Sonny in the calaboose," Tank said.

"Yep, jail for sure," Randy concurred. Jazz Man nodded in agreement.

"We've got to tell Mom and Dad what's going on," MV said.

"That'd be one dumb move," Tank said. "They'll call the law for sure and then they'll call our parents and then we'll get a switch on our behinds and orders to stay in the backyard all through Christmas."

We all paused with that summation, realizing Tank was probably correct.

"No other way, regardless," MV said. "This could be good. Mom and Dad could help us."

"How's that?" Randy asked, smashing a spider that slithered through the dirt on which we sat.

"Don't know, but a couple of adults might help us think things through," MV argued.

"We've got plenty of adults; Josh, Sonny, John I. Robertson—even Arthur. How many adults do we need? Adults screw up the world, look what's happening in Europe, tanks are rolling and war is everywhere," Tank said.

"Tank, you've got a fixation on war," I said.

"Life is war, little buddy, just look at what old man Higgins is trying to pull off, he'll close the Pullman yard," Tank shot back.

"Enough," MV said, reconsidering. "Maybe Tank's right and I'm wrong about this. We need to think long and hard—it'd be bad if Mom and Dad inadvertently interfered in our investigation," MV said.

"Inadvertently interfered?" I asked, looking at MV, surprised at her choice of some pretty interesting words.

"You're not the only person who goes to the library, Charlie," she snorted. "I say we go with Tank on this one—let's wait a while before we ask Mom and Dad to jump into this."

"Right! I'm tellin' 'ya, it would be bad," Tank said, pleased that MV was now siding with him, and Jazz Man grunted agreement. Still, MV winced—it was clear to me she wanted to tell all to Mom and Dad but Tank's warnings had caused her to be tied up in knots. For once in her life she did not know what to do.

The vote was taken and we agreed to say nothing for the moment. We said goodbye to the rest of the gang as they filed out of the Lattice Works.

When MV and I were alone I said, "I know what to do."

"You do? What's that?" MV asked, her eyes wide.

"I'll go see Calvin."

"But that would add one more adult to the mix," MV said.

"Calvin's not an adult, he's my friend. I mean, yes, he's an adult, but, golly, you know what I mean."

And MV did.

− 28 −

Tank's admonition had bothered me, to be sure—why bring another adult into our predicament? Should I actually confide to a family friend—my friend? Calvin was an adult—ancient —probably sixty years old and walked with a slight limp, assisted by a cane carved from oak. But, I knew he was a very wise man.

Calvin and his wife Eleanor owned McCoole's Men's Store on Main Street in Paddy Town. He and Eleanor played Canasta with my mom and dad and regularly came by our house for a visit every Saturday evening after their store closed at 5:00. There, listening to Saturday night radio with Mom and Dad, they let down their hair, reliving the week of retail, telling stories about customers. Stories they would never tell elsewhere, knowing Mom and Dad would never repeat them.

The bond with our family was strong and through that bond I had developed a friendship with Calvin that came about, I always thought, because he and Eleanor, a lovely, wispy, sparrow-like woman of great humor, had no children. I thought Calvin looked at me as a little guy who could be his surrogate son and Eleanor approved.

From the time I was eight I had regularly stopped by the men's store to chat seriously with Calvin—who treated me with utmost respect. I told Calvin everything about school, my ambitions in life, my fears, including my fear of Ferris wheels, and he listened intently, loving the relationship, as did I.

I walked through the front door of McCoole's Men's Store at 9:00 a.m., closing the door against the relentless wind and cold.

"Hi, Mrs. McCoole, is Calvin in?"

"He is, Charlie," Eleanor McCoole said, smiling over half-glasses from behind the checkout counter where she was recording yesterday's sales—sales that struggled through the Depression, but somehow still trickled in. "Go on back to his office if you'd like."

"Thanks, Mrs. McCoole," I said. I thought of her as Eleanor but somehow I could never call her by her first name even though I called Mr. McCoole, several years her senior, Calvin.

I trundled back through the store, past the Style Mart suits and the Bostonian shoes, turning a corner behind the shoe rack, coming to the cluttered office of Calvin McCoole, an office I loved.

I rapped on the door and heard "Enter!" from within.

I shoved the door open and saw the familiar sight—a thin, angular figure with a Sherlock Holmes pipe clenched between his teeth—Calvin McCoole—seated at his desk.

"Hi, Calvin," I said.

"Hi, Charlie," he said, pushing back from the roll-top desk from whence he ran McCoole's Men's Store. The papers on the desk seemed ready to engulf it, pennies and nickels decorated the floor where they had dropped. The room smelled of tobacco and had the easy, comfy feel of a men's club.

"Got a problem, Calvin," I said.

"Sit," Calvin said, motioning me toward a wooden chair at the side of his desk, lighting his pipe, leaning back, smiling at me, elegant in his shirt sleeves, Wembly tie, dark blue suit, slacks and suspenders. He was sartorial in dress, but was hardly a matinee idol.

As I sat I took in his physical appearance; manic gray hair that sprouted from his head like grass gone wild atop a high forehead and tiny glasses framed by those age spots old folks get. He had long legs, but one shorter than the other, a birth defect that caused him to walk with a cane.

A small smile tracked across his face as he anticipated our conversation. I smiled myself and could not help but think of last summer when I dropped by the store for a visit. Calvin had welcomed me with a wink and nod, leading me past the rows of Samsonite luggage displayed on glass shelves above the Style Mart suits, en-route to his office, assisted by his elegant oak cane, carved from, he said with yet another wink, the trunk of a tree that was 300 years old.

He nonchalantly passed gas as he led the way.

"Speak again sweet lips," he chortled, loud enough for me to hear, turning the corner past the Bostonian shoes, leaving me in the waft of the sound and smells of farts galore.

I shook my head to clear it from the aromatic memory and concentrated on the task at hand.

"Calvin, should we tell our parents?"

"Tell 'em what, Charlie?" he asked in a swirl of pipe smoke that encased his head.

"Well," I began, and spilled the story, the whole story—everything but the part about Arthur—even Calvin would have had a hard time with that.

Calvin's eyebrows went up several times as I related the adventures of the Maple Avenue Gang. He leaned forward when I mentioned RJ Higgins and re-loaded his pipe when I reported on the contents of the envelope that Miss Harriett Keyser had entrusted to Ralston Bazzle.

I finished and Calvin puffed on his pipe, saying nothing.

"Calvin, what should we do?"

"You know what to do, Charlie."

"No, no, I don't, that's why I came down here to talk with you."

"Charlie, you're a smart young man. You know you should tell your parents what you and your friends have gotten into."

"Yeah, but Tank says we have enough adults involved now, and with all due respect, he says more adults will really screw this up."

"Tank? Tank told you this?"

"Yep, said we should keep quiet and handle this ourselves."

"Well, Tank's an impressive young fellow, but I think he's in error this time. Tell me, who have you known and trusted all your life, Tank or your mom and dad?"

"Well, when you put it that way," I said.

"Tell your parents, tell them everything" Calvin said, winking once more at me, knocking the bowl of his pipe in the large ashtray on his desk, ashes flying onto the floor.

"Okay, if you're sure we should bring them into this..."

"Charlie, you just brought me into this."

"Yeah, but, you're Calvin, you're—you're not an adult, I mean, you, you're—my friend…"

Calvin leaned forward and put a hand on my shoulder. "A better compliment I could never receive, Charlie. Now, go, tell your mom and dad—like I said—tell them everything."

— 29 —

MV and I headed for the living room where Mom and Dad
continued to inventory belongings to see if the two hoboes
who had been in the house had stolen anything besides the
suit jacket and tie.

"You did what?" Mom said, anger in her voice. "You took
your daddy's jacket and tie and gave it to a hobo?"

Dad and Mom sat on the blue couch in the living room and
MV and I stood facing them, the fireplace to our backs, the
Christmas tree to our left. I was conscious of a picture of the
Virgin Mary on the wall space at the bottom of the staircase
to our right. I hoped she was giving us special dispensation
in regard to our actions.

Dad said nothing, but his look said it all. With all due respect
to Calvin, Tank may have been right.

MV took control. She had related the entire story as our
parents sat, entranced. It was obvious they could not believe

what they were hearing; two hoboes, one an attorney, the other acting as his legal assistant; then there was the Scarface man who had accosted us. Our parents obviously found it all hard to believe but knowing we would never lie to them, their disbelief evolved to serious concern for our wellbeing and a need to thwart the nefarious actions of RJ Higgins. I noted MV had left out the part about Arthur; a wise choice.

"Mom, Dad, please listen to us. We did something wrong, we know; we went to the Pullman yard when you told us we could not. That was bad. But some real good has come out of that. Our gang found Miss Keyser's satchel and letter and we're trying to right a wrong. Josh and Sonny are good guys—they're putting themselves in jeopardy to help us," MV pleaded.

There was that word again—"Jeperdy." I was impressed, as always, by my sister. She was not only using big words, she was making a big impression on our parents, I could tell, seeing my dad's features soften.

MV ended her spiel and we waited. Mom said, "Well, I swan. I just can't believe you two are involved in something like this. Bill, what are we going to do?"

MV and I turned our heads in unison. My dad's beefy forearms were on his lap, his hands, intertwined, his thumbs twirling. We waited but he said nothing.

"Daddy?" MV said.

Dad glanced from us to Mom and said, "I think we need to listen to the kids. There's a chance here to stop Higgins from turning our backyard into a cesspool of garbage. That's good enough for me. What can we do to help?" Dad asked us.

Well, here was a unique development; my dad asking us what he could do to help. I have to be honest, that had never occurred before. Dad made the rules and we followed them, a practice that worked just fine for me; it was a simple approach to life and there were no questions to ask. But give advice to Dad? I couldn't quite grasp the concept.

No problem, however, for MV.

"Here's the way I see it, Daddy," MV began. "RJ Higgins is a Mason and he'll be at the Christmas Dinner at noon today, right?"

"Without question," Dad affirmed, his thumbs twirling once more.

"Can you start up a conversation that will let him know the rumor on the railroad is that someone stole something from the Pullman yard—looked like a small black satchel?"

"Sure, but if RJ thinks somebody has the satchel, he might go berserk, try to kill somebody," Dad said.

"Yeah, but he won't know who to kill," MV said.

Dad smiled. "Get him to react, huh? See if RJ has a small explosion. If he does, we'll know he's probably guilty of altering the will."

"That's what I'm thinking, Daddy. How can we do it?"

"Bill, this sounds dangerous to me," Mom interjected. "If

there is something afoot and RJ suspects you know something," Mom said, hesitating, "he might try to harm you. Remember, there's the Scarface man." Mom's anxiety was obviously increasing as the moments passed.

"I don't think RJ will suspect anything, Mabel, if my story is good enough."

"I think it'll work," MV said. "You could say you thought RJ should know that some railroader at the Beanery said he saw a suspicious person trespassing on Higgins' property earlier this week. Tell him the person was toting a leather bag and ran when he was spotted," MV said, her arms crossed, her foot tapping the floor.

I have to tell you, my sister had style.

"RJ will want to know who the railroader is," Mom cautioned.

"No way for me to know, just gossip from the railroad boys down at the Beanery," Dad replied, "might do the trick, get him to thinking, it might work."

"Just a minute," Mom said, this time her foot stomping the floor. "This is a lie. We live our lives always striving to be free of lies and deceit. How can you condone this, Bill?" Mom said, her voice rising slightly.

Dad placed his hand on Mom's hand and said, "I agree with your mother, kids." My heart sank and MV let loose a sigh. Dad then added, looking at Mom, "But sometimes a small fib can right a great wrong. If we truly suspect that RJ Higgins has committed a heinous act such as Mary Virginia and Charlie describe, a conclusion backed up by John I. Robertson, then it would be a crime on our part not to act."

Mom seemed to have an internal quandary; she closed her eyes and sought help from above. She alternately frowned and fluttered her eyelashes and then, finally, squeezed Dad's hand, "I guess you're right," she said, the worry on her face intensifying, "but we need to get in touch with John I. to see what he has to say."

Dad leaned over, kissed Mom and stroked her hair. He then voiced agreement with her assertion and announced that he was going upstairs to don his second favorite suit and tie. He came back downstairs within fifteen minutes and kissed Mom goodbye, saying he would meet her at the Masonic Lodge at noon. He walked through the last of the remaining snow in the backyard and threw open the garage door. A few moments later he backed our 1932 Ford out of the garage and set off for John I. Robertson's law offices, down near the courthouse.

— 30 —

It was high noon on Christmas Eve and Tank and I were headed to the Mineral County Library. Tank carried in his Schwinn basket the real estate volume we had 'checked out' for Josh's review. I rode beside him on the Hawthorne. The book would go back into the library in reverse; Tank would put it in the window well and I would reach through and retrieve the volume, replacing it in the stacks. This one would be easy, given Tank's long reach.

"Meet me around the side of the building; give me five minutes, and I'll open the window. Just shove the book through to me. I'll be right back," I instructed as Tank nodded that he understood.

"Afternoon, Miss Church," I sang out as I entered the library, feeling the rush of warm air.

"Oh, Charlie, hello. I wonder if you would do me a favor?"

"Sure, Miss Church, what is it?"

"See that stack of books over there? Would you mind taking them back to the reading room in the annex area? My lumbago has me in a fix and I don't want to be carrying any more weight than I have to," she explained.

"I'd be glad to, Miss Church," I said, moving toward the pile of nine or ten heavy books on a table near the entrance to the library.

"Thank you, Charlie, you're very nice to help me. Thanks to you, I'll be able to close up at noon so I can catch the start of the Christmas Eve street fair."

"Yes, ma'am. I want to do that, too. Should be a fun time. Big crowd's gatherin' downtown," I said.

"I'm taking the grandchildren, they want to ride the Ferris wheel," she said, smiling.

I shuddered at her mention of the Ferris wheel, a thing of torture. I lifted the pile of books and walked through the main section of the complex of rooms, on into the annex reading room, where few people went. I switched on the light and looked around for a place to put the books. All the tables were full so I put the books on the floor and, two-by-two, began to place them on the ledge that jutted out of the wall halfway to the ceiling. Doing so I had a feeling there was something within my vision that I somehow could not see. It was perplexing and that bothered me a great deal as I loaded all ten books on the ledge. I stood back and looked. "What was out of place?" I wondered.

The wall was smooth with little fissures in it. I followed the pattern in the surface before me and I closed one eye, as though I were aiming a rifle. Nothing. I refocused and then closed the other eye. Something was odd. Finally, it hit me. The rivulets seemed to sink inward near the middle of the wall. I pulled over a chair and climbed up on it so I could look down on the ledge that now held the books. I ran my hand along the ledge and felt an indentation.

I slipped my fingers into the slot and pulled up. There was a sensation that something had moved but the surface was still intact. I pulled again, this time very hard. The ledge cracked and splintered and dust filled the air. My first thought was that this was another Alcatraz thing; I surely would end up in prison for destroying public property. And then I saw it. It was at least twelve inches long and two or three inches in circumference—a steel cylinder protruding from its entombment in the wall.

I looked around to make certain I was alone and gently pulled the container from its resting place. I laid it on the floor and examined it. One end of the cylinder had a cap that screwed off. I twisted the top. At first, it resisted, seeming to not want to be opened. Another twist and the cap moved. Three more turns and it was off. I reached in the container and pulled out a thick, rolled document. I unfolded it. The letters stared straight up at me, "Last Will & Testament of Harriett Keyser."

"Charlie, are you back there?" Miss Church called, startling me.

"Yes, ma'am," I responded, rolling up the document and stuffing it back in the cylinder, stepping down off the chair, moving toward the door, shouting that all was in order.

"Alright, Charlie, thank you!" Miss Church said.

I stepped back into the room and opened the cylinder once again, fearing I had made a mistake, intent on reviewing what I thought I had seen. The same words stared at me—and I realized it made sense; the county library was a special place for Miss Keyser. She had supported the library annually with sizeable gifts. There was even a plaque on the front wall thanking her for her friendship. She was here often, and here is where, by golly, she had hidden her real will. I smiled to myself, satisfied I had found Miss Keyser's original document, and shivered in excitement. I returned the will to the cylinder, only then remembering that Tank was at the well, waiting to pass to me the real estate book that had to be placed back in its proper place.

Suddenly aware I was far beyond the five minutes I had carved out for the book-return project, I ran to the next room. I dragged the large wooden stool I had used once before to the window well, climbed to the window, opened it, and looked for Tank.

"Are you out there?" I hissed through the window. The only reply was a grunt and the shuffle of Tank's feet in the slosh of melting snow. "I found the will! Harriet Keyser's will, Tank! She hid it here, in the library! Here, take it and meet me at the front entrance!" I whispered, shoving the cylinder through the window, using both hands to toss it upward where I heard it clang onto the street and saw Tank's feet move toward it, spraying water at me. I heard another grunt and I knew Tank had the cylinder.

In my excitement at having found the will, I forgot completely about retrieving the real estate volume from Tank. Too late, he was gone. Returning the book would have to wait. I quickly closed the window, used my coat sleeve to wipe off the sill, climbed down off the stool, returned it to its original spot, and walked briskly toward the library's front door, saying my goodbyes to Miss Church.

"Bye, bye, Charlie, thank you again, and Merry Christmas!" Miss Church called after me as she locked the door of the library, intent on heading for the grandkids and the Ferris wheel. I landed on my Hawthorne at the library entrance as she walked away and rushed to the side of the yellow building where Tank was waiting on his Schwinn—by the window well where I once was trapped until Tank had pulled me free.

"Let's go!" I shouted at Tank, who simply stood still, straddling his bike.

"What about this?" he asked, waving the real estate volume at me.

"Sorry—I forgot about it when I found the cylinder."

"What cylinder?" Tank asked, frowning.

"The cylinder I just threw out the window to you, doofus!"

"I don't know what you're talkin' about," Tank said, raising both arms in exasperation, throwing the real estate book in the basket of his bike, "I just got here. You said five minutes—I waited five minutes and then went back to the front of the building and waited for you. Then I came back here, waiting for that window to open, which it never did!" he hissed at me.

"You—you don't have the cylinder?"

"All I have, Charlie, is the real estate book. Like I said, I waited fifteen minutes out front for you and then I came back around here to the side of the building, waiting for you to open that window," Tank said, pointing to the window in the well where his feet bisected the Schwinn, his shoes firmly planted on the concrete sidewalk. I flashed back to the cylinder toss and realized that Tank's shoes were not the ones I had seen. Those shoes were work boots, not Tank's street shoes. And the sound I had heard was not Tank's voice—it was only a grunt—a grunt anyone could have made.

Someone had the cylinder and Harriett Keyser's will and it wasn't Tank. We were screwed.

Not knowing what else to do, I explained the dilemma to Tank. He shrugged and, once again took command, suggesting we ride the streets to see if we could find anyone that might be carrying a metal cylinder.

"Needle in a haystack," I said.

"Got any better idea?" he asked.

"Nope," I said, and we turned our bikes toward downtown and the Christmas street fair that was growing larger by the moment. We rode off as "Good King Wenceslas" drifted through the air, knowing our chances of ever seeing the cylinder again were slim to none.

Across the street from the yellow grade school and its basement library, behind a snow-covered sign that said "Grace Methodist Church", watching our every move, was a sneering man with a large red scar on his face.

In his hand he held a metal cylinder.

− 31 −

The Masonic Lodge was crowded; at least fifty couples were in attendance at the annual Christmas Eve Dinner. Dad and Mom chatted with Calvin McCoole who asked how I was doing, eyebrows raised. Dad assured him I was fine and then spotted RJ Higgins at the punch bowl across the room.

"Good to see you, Calvin, give my best to Eleanor," Dad said, shifting toward RJ Higgins.

"Nice to see you, Bill, hope Charlie's keeping you up to date on everything," Calvin said, turning toward a fellow merchant who wanted to discuss a Chamber of Commerce issue.

Dad wondered what Calvin meant by the reference to me but lost the thought as he focused on RJ Higgins' considerable paunch hovering over the punch bowl table, his beady eyes darting from one person to the other as he poured whiskey from a flask into his half-full cup.

"Whoa, RJ, that's a pretty stiff dinner drink you're pouring," Dad said, smiling, as he sauntered up to the town's least-liked figure.

"Huh? Oh, Ryan, want one?"

"No, never touch the stuff. Used to, but I couldn't handle it. Still smells good though," Dad said.

"Yeah, well, good 'ta see 'ya Ryan," RJ said, moving away.

"RJ, something you should know."

Higgins stopped and looked back.

"Yeah?"

"Some boys over at the Beanery were sayin' they saw someone trespassing on your property the other day. That Pullman car acreage you own."

RJ was all ears. "Really? Did they say what he looked like?"

"Nope, just said some hobo was running like a bat out of hades—said he was carryin' a leather satchel of some sort."

RJ's jaw dropped and his cup of punch fell from his hand, splashing its contents across the Masonic Lodge floor. RJ grabbed Dad by the lapels of his jacket, looked up at him, and muttered in a threatening manner, "Tell me who saw him, Ryan, I want to know what the lousy thief stole from my property. Tell me!"

Dad's large fists tightened firmly around RJ's hands as he looked down into what could only be described as an evil face. He squeezed Higgins' hands—hard. The little man's face contorted with pain as his grip was loosened by the hefty railroader. "Tell you what, RJ, if you're that excited about what I thought was petty thievery you must have something very valuable hidden in those Pullman cars," Dad said.

"Course not," RJ countered, trying to gain control of himself, rubbing his hand as Dad loosened his grip. "Just don't want anybody messin' with what's mine, that's all. Tell the boys at the Beanery there's a $100 reward if anybody can tell me who the thief is," RJ said, and rushed from the Lodge.

Watching it all and seeing RJ's hasty exit, John I. Robertson walked across the room to Dad, his eyebrows lifted, a frown on his face. "I'd say our man was mighty upset," he said.

"That's putting it mildly. He offered a $100 reward for anyone who could identify the thief," Dad replied.

"Don't say," John I. said, his hands pulling on his suspender straps. "Guess I'll need to get over to the police station and bring Chief Dawson up to speed on this. He needs to put a watch on Higgins."

— *32* —

RJ Higgins tore down the steps of the Masonic Lodge with a vengeance. He exited the building on Main Street, ran down the sidewalk and yanked the door to his Hudson open. He quickly pushed the car's starter button, slammed the door closed, put the car in gear and stepped hard on the gas pedal. The Hudson screamed from its parking space, startling pedestrians who jumped from its path, showering some with cinder-filled remnants of snow.

RJ drove straight toward the hobo jungle near the Pullman graveyard. He parked his Hudson a street away, grabbed an overcoat from the back seat of the car, tugged at his bulging vest, loosened his tie, and began his trek through the woods that formed a barrier to the jungle. He emerged in a clearing that served as a small village for the hoboes that lived in the three acres of space. He had been here several times before when he had deposited a drunk Rembrandt Simmons in pretty much the same spot where he now stood, gazing into the compound.

Approximately half of the sixty or so folks that lived in the tent camp were mulling around the area of several open fires in barrels, a Depression Christmas Eve celebration of sorts was underway; ill-clothed children played in wet snow that was rapidly vanishing, a crate of oranges was being hovered over by several women, and four men were playing cards beside a campfire. The card players stopped their game and stared at RJ as he approached their circle.

"RJ Higgins, here. Some of you probably know me. Rem Simmons does some work for me—you know, Scarface," RJ said, sauntering up to the card players in an authoritative manner, spitting into the fire in the barrel. "Lookin' for someone who found a black satchel over there in the Pullman yard," RJ advised, his thumb beckoning over his shoulder. "I've got a hundred dollar bill for anybody that can tell me who it was."

"What kinda' satchel?" a card player said, spitting a wad of tobacco at RJ's feet, turning a patch of snow a dirty brown.

"Don't know, thought maybe you boys could tell me," RJ responded, stepping back from the plug.

"So—you've got a hundred dollars on you?" a second hobo asked, looking up from the now stalled card game, smiling in what could only be described as a threatening manner.

"Sure do," RJ said, spreading his overcoat, opening his vest, button by button, revealing a holster and .38 revolver. "Got a hundred dollars in my pocket and Mr. Smith and Mr. Wesson close to my heart," he grunted, returning the smile.

The card game resumed. All heads looked down. No help was offered.

"Tell Rem to get over to my office soon as you see him, and—Merry Christmas," RJ hissed, sarcasm dripping, tossing the $100 bill on the makeshift card table. "Split the hundred four ways, boys, and remember my friends Smith & Wesson if you start to get greedy."

The man with bushy eyebrows and menacing stare stomped out of the yard, feeling eyes on his back and his .38 against his chest.

— 33 —

Ten minutes later RJ pulled into his driveway on Carskadon Hill and came to a screeching stop. He pulled the key from the Hudson's ignition as Rembrandt Simmons walked around the corner of the house.

"Rem!" RJ practically screamed as he stepped from the car, slamming the door hard. "I've been looking for you!"

Simmon's face broke into a sinister grin, heightening the redness of the scar that sliced down his face. "Been lookin' for you, too, RJ, and I think you're gonna' be mighty interested in this little piece of information in this here cylinder," Scarface said, holding high a metal container.

"Inside," RJ scowled, unlocking his office door, walking into the foyer. Scarface followed, making sure he gave a good swift kick into the ribs of Briggs the dog. The dog howled in pain and retreated to the end of the foyer, near the front door, seeking an escape. This time RJ ignored the attack on Briggs,went straight to his liquor cabinet, and poured three fingers of whiskey into each of two glasses.

RJ took a large gulp of liquor from his glass and handed Scarface the other tumbler, glowering at him. Scarface placed the metal container under his arm and, with the other arm, reached for the glass. He emptied it with one long swallow, followed by a murmur of pleasure as the whiskey warmed his throat. He shoved the glass forward, signaling for a refill, and RJ complied. Scarface lifted the glass and repeated his quick disposal of another three fingers of whiskey, giving him a full buzz.

"Well?" RJ said.

"Got Harriett Keyser's will, RJ—right here in this cylinder," Scarface said, fondling the container, swaying slightly.

"What? You've got it? How? Where did you get it? Show me!" RJ said, walking behind his mammoth desk, easing into his office chair.

"Details, you want details?" Scarface asked in a mocking fashion, grabbing the bottle of whiskey from the sideboard where RJ had left it, sliding into one of the leather chairs facing RJ's desk, his words beginning to slur just a bit. "You wanted the old lady's will and I've got it, that's all."

"Your search in the Pullman yard—the satchel—you found it in the yard?"

"Don't make no difference where I found it, point is, I got it," Simmons replied, pouring himself yet another drink.

"All I see is a metal cylinder, Rem. You've got no satchel and my bet is you don't have Harriett Keyser's will."

"Says you—will's in the cylinder."

"Prove it, show it to me."

Scarface opened the cylinder, pulled the will from the container and held it up as RJ leaned forward across his desk and read the words on the page Scarface held. There was no doubt—it was the real will, RJ realized, feeling a rush of excitement.

"Where'd you find that?" RJ asked as Scarface pushed the will back into the metal container setting it next to the bottle of whiskey on the edge of the broad desk that separated him and RJ.

"You were right on one thing," Scarface replied, "the satchel was in one of the Pullman cars. Buncha' kids from over on Maple Avenue found the bag. I was sleepin' one off in the car. They woke me up and I seen 'em find it. Little punks hit me with a brick and ran. I been followin' 'em every day—one of 'em found the cylinder in the county library and I took it from 'em."

RJ flashed back to Harriett Keyser's beneficence toward the Mineral County Library and realized it was abundantly clear; she was in the library several times every week, she must have hidden the will and cylinder somewhere in the stacks in the yellow grade school basement.

"A thousand dollars, Rem—you've earned it. Give me the will and you'll have a big payday," RJ said, sitting behind his large desk, pulling a stack of bills from a middle desk drawer that he held open.

"Sure 'nuff," big payday. Bigger than you think, RJ. I'll need five thousand dollars for this here cylinder and its contents."

RJ's eyes narrowed to slits and he said nothing.

Thirty seconds of silence engulfed the room as the two men stared at one another.

"Well?" Scarface said, looking away, breaking the stare between him and RJ.

"Rem, if you think you can come in here and extort an ungodly sum from me, you are badly mistaken, my friend," RJ said.

"Five thousand—or no will, RJ," Scarface countered.

RJ's hand moved slowly to his vest where he loosened two buttons. His hammy fist came to a rest for a second time that day on his Smith and Wesson. He brought the pistol into the open, pointing it at Scarface's chest.

"Seems I was here in my office, Rem, when I was rudely accosted by a burglar—one of those Yeggs from the hobo yard. The slime had been drinking, whiskey on his breath. He lunged at me as he came through the door, Rem. All I could do, I'll tell Chief Dawson, was grab this here Smith and Wesson and protect myself. Shame. Blood all over the floor. 'Goodness sakes,' Chief Dawson will think, 'poor RJ Higgins, rich man, set upon by this Yegg intent on stealin' the rich man's money.' It'll play real well with the Chief and it'll read even better in *The Paddy Town Daily News*," RJ said, exhibiting a threatening smile through the slits beneath large and bushy eyebrows. Rem heard the words through a fog of rye whiskey. His nerve suddenly bolstered by the alcohol, he leaned forward, extending his hand toward the bottle. RJ's eyes followed his move. Scarface's hand hovered momentarily and suddenly swerved toward the metal container that held the will. He swept the cylinder from the desk and in one swift motion set it sailing toward RJ Higgins' sizeable head. RJ sprawled backward as the canister cut deeply into his forehead, causing blood to gush, immediately rendering him unconscious.

Briggs the dog stood in the doorway of the office watching the attack on his master, a slow, guttural growl rising in his throat.

Scarface stood up, blinked hard, and steadied himself on the desk. "Blood everywhere, RJ, just like you said. Only it's yours, not mine," he giggled, and then moved hesitantly around the desk, his mind still blurred from the whiskey. Pushing RJ out of his desk chair and onto the floor, Scarface rummaged through the open middle desk drawer where he found an envelope marked "Seasonal Ferris wheel Receipts". In the envelope was $8,000 cash.

Rem smiled to himself, grabbed the envelope and stooped to pick up the cylinder from the floor. He looked around for something with which to wipe off the blood that covered the container and, standing erect with a wobble, selected RJ's partially opened vest as a cleaning cloth. Wiping the cylinder clean, he opened the canister and inserted beside the Keyser will the envelope full of cash he had just stolen. He then tightly closed the cap of the container and let his eyes fall on the .38 that had toppled out of RJ's hand and onto his desk.

Rem picked up the gun and slid it in his trouser pocket. He thought about another shot of whiskey but the adrenalin had partially cleared the state he had been in; for the first time since he had entered the room he felt a stab of regret—he had gone too far. RJ, if he weren't dead, would find him and kill him. Rem's immediate thought was to flee. He backed out of the room and into the foyer, almost falling over Briggs the dog.

Scarface turned, cursed the growling dog and kicked for his ribs. This time Briggs was ready and quickly moved aside, causing Scarface to lose his balance and fall to the floor. Cursing himself and the dog, he crawled to his knees, stood on shaky legs, and returned to RJ's office where he grabbed a fresh bottle of whiskey from the liquor cabinet. He returned to the foyer, again encountering the dog. Scarface went for Briggs' body, lashing out with three swift kicks, connecting this time, causing Briggs to howl in pain. Scarface laughed, threw back the front door, leaving it wide open, and ran from the building and into wet woods—fleeing Carskadon Hill, intent on hopping a freight out of town.

He did not see Briggs bound from the porch and follow him into the woods.

— 34 —

We slowed our bikes as we neared the center of the Christmas fair where a considerable crowd had gathered as temperatures warmed and snow disappeared. The large lot was bone dry from the afternoon sun and a throng of people populated the area, intent on a Christmas celebration. Tank and I got off our bikes and pushed them through the crowd, acknowledging both kids my age and older folks who were friends of our families. Conversations ensued and we eyed every passer-by, hoping to see someone toting a metal cylinder—the needle in this human haystack.

I forced my way through the clogged street as carefully as I could, apologizing as my bike pushed against the people in the crowd, gathering some frowns from the adults. Against my better judgment, Tank and I opted to check out the service area behind the beer joint on the adjacent corner, back by the trash bins, and out of sight from the crowd. We found ourselves next to the main Baltimore & Ohio line where hoboes often hopped freights leaving town. Here the snow residue remained and melting ice had created pools of dirty water filled with cinders from freight trains. We had gone only a few steps in the secluded area when Scarface stepped from behind one of the large bins, a gun in one hand, a fifth of whiskey in the other.

"Snot-nosed kids. You're the reason I'm in a fix and you're gonna' pay 'fore I leave this burg," he said, obviously drunk.

"Whoa, whoa, steady," Tank said, holding his arms in the air as though it was a stickup.

Scarface staggered slightly and fell sideways, hitting a pool of water and cinders beside the trash bin. A metal cylinder toppled from his belt and fell to the ground.

"The cylinder! He's got the cylinder!" I cried, immediately wishing I had not done so.

"That's right," Scarface wheezed from his prone position as he grabbed the cylinder, holding it aloft, laughing, coiled, ready to strike. "Got the will, got the cash, got rid of old man Higgins, and now I got me two of the brats that have caused all the trouble," Scarface said, stumbling to his feet, advancing toward us, pistol extended, clothes wet, cinders imbedded in his cheek.

From the corner of my eye I saw something flash. Scarface did not see it coming. A huge black dog was flying through the air, fangs bared, striking Scarface with tremendous force, jaws open, then tightly snapped shut, teeth imbedding deeply into Rembrandt Simmons' right buttock, a dog intent on tearing flesh from bone. Scarface swung around, screaming, and pointed the gun at the dog, only to go limp from pain, dropping the pistol. Tank lost no time, taking full advantage of the canine attack, grabbing the cylinder as Scarface lost consciousness.

The dog, a giant black schnauzer, released his grip and Scarface fell to the wet ground like a rag doll. The dog looked down at his tormentor and tilted his head to one side. He then turned toward me and I backed away, thinking we had a rabid animal on our hands. I froze as the large schnauzer, dripping water, walked calmly toward me and sat at my feet. He looked up at me and blinked large brown, beautiful eyes, as though trying to explain his actions. I knew then and there that MV and I were not the only ones who had borne the brunt of Scarface's perversity.

I knelt down and comforted the dog, rubbing behind his ears, while Tank tossed Scarface's pistol into the garbage bin. The dog looked one more time at the now silent Scarface and emitted a long, low growl. He then turned, licked my face, and sauntered off into the night. Revenge was his.

I watched the giant schnauzer disappear around the corner and turned to Tank, who was opening the cylinder to inspect the will. He pulled the document from the container and arched his eyebrows in surprise as yet another document followed the will; an envelope flopped out, spilling one hundred-dollar bills on the ground and into the slush.

"What did Scarface mean when he said he had gotten old man Higgins?" I asked Tank, still shaking from the turn of events, wondering why there was money in the cylinder.

"Don't know," Tank said, retrieving the envelope, gathering up the soaked bills that had fallen. "But we've got the container and the will—and lots of money—in an envelope marked

'Ferris wheel Seasonal Receipts,' " Tank read. "We need to find John I. Robertson and the police. I'll bet old man Higgins has been robbed—if not worse," Tank said, fully in control of the situation.

"Right, let's go," I said, mounting my bike, hearing RJ Higgins' carousel calliope begin to blare Christmas music at the hub of the growing crowd moving from the street fair toward his Ferris wheel and carousel.

"Hold on, hold on," Tank snapped, "let's see how much is here." Tank pulled the rest of the cash out of the envelope, taking care to not disturb the will. Taking his time, he counted the money. He whistled softly and stuffed the cash back in the cylinder, snapping it shut. "I count $8,000," he said.

"Eight thousand dollars? That's a fortune!" I said.

A threatening voice from behind us startled both Tank and me.

"A fortune—and it's mine!" the voice hissed and Scarface was on his feet, blood seeping from his torn buttock. It was clear that trauma had sobered him up and he was again dangerous, this time armed with a switchblade knife that he waved in a circular motion, moving toward us.

He advanced toward Tank, brushing past me with a hard shove. The Hawthorne went out from under me and I hit the slush and cinders. I scrambled from under the bike just as Scarface lunged for Tank, who caught him on the fly, wresting the canister away from his attacker. The cylinder came flying toward me. I caught it on the run and broke for the crowds in the Ferris wheel lot, sloshing through melting snow and water. Scarface regained his footing as Tank rushed in for the kill. Scarface easily eluded him and, knife in hand, my personal tyrant came chasing after me.

I raced toward the crowd and ran straight into a golden retriever being walked by the local jeweler, John Rinard. I went upside down, leaving a combination of dirt, cinders and nasty water on Mr. Rinard and regained my footing. But the cylinder was gone. I was frantic, searching for the metal container that was nowhere in sight. Scarface was rushing toward me, past the circling carousel that continued to blast Christmas carols into the air.

He struck me from behind, the impact to my lower back and legs driving me like a cannonball through a crowd of startled onlookers who seemed stunned and frozen in place as the scene exploded before them. I landed amidst a forest of shoes that trod the Ferris wheel grounds. In front of my nose was the canister. I grabbed it and regained my footing, only to be hit from behind once again by a relentless Scarface.

This impact was again solid and it catapulted me toward the base of the Ferris wheel. I hit the ground with a thud but quickly clambered to my feet and ran, holding the canister tightly. I held my breath and seeing the Ferris wheel was not moving, jumped into one of its gondolas for cover. The toe of the shoe on my right foot hit the lynchpin on the operator's control system as I literally flew through the air and the wheel suddenly began to move—the terrifying machine had me trapped, carrying me upward, upward to the sky. I froze in fear but managed to grab the side of the gondola as the ground disappeared before me; I was now in the bosom of the terrifying turning wheel. I turned in despair, seeking an escape route, and saw him; two gondolas behind me was Scarface, staring at me, climbing toward me, grinning an evil grin, intent on carrying the chase to the very end.

I looked down; far below was the Maple Avenue Gang, arriving one by one on their bikes. MV was as terrified as I when she saw me peer out over the side of the rising gondola

"Charlie!" she shouted, "Come down from there!"

"If only I could," I thought, petrified.

— 35 —

The wheel lurched as I reached the very top of the arc, and I knew the gondola I was in was poised to plummet toward the earth. Hundreds of heads were turned toward me. I frantically surveyed the crowd below and saw RJ Higgins pushing his way through the crowd toward the wheel's operator's bench, knocking bystanders to the ground, shaking his fist toward his wheel, shouting obscenities. His clothes were covered in blood and he had a crazed look on his face as he marched to the operator's platform and took control of the Ferris wheel.

"We Three Kings of Orient Are" blasted from the calliope and drifted upward toward me, engulfing me, creating a bizarre feeling of operatic drama.

My gondola was swinging back and forth and I thought I might be sick. Then I remembered that Munch said I would pee my pants if I were ever again on the Ferris wheel, and I found new resolve.

My concern of falling or peeing was quickly replaced by a fear of being thrown off the "Pleasure" wheel as I realized

Scarface, on the framework of the wheel, was slowly inching toward me. The calliope music filled the night and I shoved the cylinder in the waist of my trousers, crawling out onto the spokes as the wheel began its descent down toward the ground, just as Scarface entered my gondola car. He grabbed my trouser leg and I gave as forceful a kick as I could muster. Scarface lost his balance and fell backward into the car, giving me some leeway.

A scream from below knifed through the chaotic din, telling me my mother had arrived on the Ferris wheel grounds.

Sirens began to wail in the background; John I. Robertson had found Chief Dawson.

RJ Higgins worked feverishly at the control platform, alternately slowing and accelerating the wheel, intent on taking his revenge on Scarface and finishing me in the process. "Please," I thought, "stop the wheel!" when, for the second time this Christmas, a knife whizzed by my head. It stuck in the wooden bar of the gondola next to me, rattling back and forth in the socket it had created. I panicked, threw caution aside and climbed as fast as I could toward the center of the wheel. Looking down, I could not believe my eyes; MV had climbed aboard the rotating monster as it slowed. She was on the framework of the wheel, climbing toward me. My mother, looking up, screamed again—louder.

Scarface saw RJ Higgins glowering from the operator's platform, staring upward toward him. "He's got Harriett Keyser's will!" Scarface yelled at the top of his lungs, overriding the calliope noise, pointing at me as the wheel accelerated.

"He's got the cylinder! The will!" And Scarface laughed hysterically.

Higgins froze, looking around to see hundreds of people glued to the action—hundreds who must have heard Scarface scream Harriet Keyser's name. Wondering who in the crowd might be putting two and two together, Higgins raised his fist at Scarface, cursing him, shouting, "Hold your tongue you idiot!"—and pushed the wheel to its fastest speed.

RJ was caught by surprise when my dad bounded onto the platform, grabbing him by the collar, lifting him straight off the floor. A giant red-bearded man coming at Higgins from the left followed Dad. The two scooped RJ from the operator's bench, pulling his hands from the throttle, but not before RJ jammed the wheel, locking it into position at its fastest revolution just as my gondola skimmed the lowest portion of its turn and again began to climb skyward.

Sonny Longsten ran to assist Dad and Josh. He ripped heavy rope from the metal eyelets used for crowd control around the Ferris wheel and tied a shouting, cursing Higgins to the metal frame that housed the wheel's motor. The crowd roared its approval as it witnessed Higgins being subdued and then let out a collective gasp as the Ferris wheel's rotation began to blur before their eyes, faster and faster.

MV climbed higher as the wheel roared at twice its normal speed. She reached out for Scarface's foot above her and Scarface, winded, grabbed and clung to a spoke near the gondola where his imbedded knife protruded from its wooden resting place. He pulled the knife from the gondola surface just as MV yanked his foot off the spoke where his weight was centered. Both Scarface and MV went flying through twenty feet of air, falling into yet another gondola, heavy winter clothing breaking their fall.

The calliope music blared "We Three Kings" incessantly as life or death played out. Uplifted faces were captivated by the high drama.

The wheel suddenly shuddered as Josh Wenning bounded once more to the operator's bench, giving the regulator stick a huge kick, loosening it from its jammed position. I straddled the frame of the wheel as it slowed too quickly, causing it to spasmodically stutter and shake. I fell backward as a violent spasm grabbed the wheel and the cylinder slipped from my waistband, falling through the air, landing in the gondola where Scarface and MV battled. I clung for dear life to the wheel's spokes that whipped back and forth like taut rubber bands. Shaking my head, regaining balance, I began to work my way toward MV as she struggled with Scarface, punching him repeatedly with her little fists and feet while the turning, quivering wheel tossed them about. I said a prayer and jumped from the undulating spoke into the passenger gondola where MV was fighting for her life. I fell, terrified, toward the swinging car, and landed hard on Scarface's back. He quickly turned his attention from MV to me, grabbed me by the neck, and slammed me to the floor of the gondola as the blaring calliope choreographing our harrowing dance came to an abrupt silence.

I was dazed from the impact and the sudden quiet. Scarface's bony knees dug into my body, pinning my shoulders, his knife at my throat; through the haze I realized his intention was to swipe the blade across my jugular. Sensing he was going to win the battle, he grinned down at me with hatred in his eyes. I waited for the searing wound and blood that would follow when, without warning, Scarface's eyes bulged and he screamed. MV had grabbed the cylinder from the floor of the gondola and, holding to the Ferris wheel's rigging, slammed the cylinder down hard, attempting to smash Scarface's hand. Scarface's scream was followed by a maniacal laugh as he reached back, grabbing MV's arm, pulling him toward her, pushing her down beside me. We were, I realized, both goners. I saw the hate in Scarface's eyes as he raised his arm, knife in hand, preparing to strike.

From out of nowhere, there was Arthur, standing on the frame of the Ferris wheel with total balance, his porter's uniform resplendent, his bold red necktie flying in the wind, the wheel shaking wildly. Arthur's large hand engulfed Scarface's arm, closing with such force I heard bone crushing. Scarface screamed as Arthur picked him bodily from the gondola, hurling him downward. The crowd below recoiled in terror, watching with fascination.

Scarface bounced along the frame of the wheel, his body finally dropping to the ground, causing onlookers to scatter, avoiding both him and his knife that had careened from his hand, clanging onto the roof of Chief Dawson's cruiser.

Scarface lay motionless, sprawled on the ground. Then, amazingly, he slowly struggled to his feet, cursing aloud, and was off and running; but only for a short distance as Tank, Randy and Munch moved to block his path. Our assailant made one last screaming protest, dodging the three of them as onlookers separated in fright, giving Scarface a clear line of escape. He did not count on Calvin McCoole's cane as it extended from the line of spectators, tripping Scarface, sending him flying, landing with a resounding thud.

Tank took command, jumping on Scarface, pushing his captive's face into the dirt, holding him for the police whose sirens continued to punctuate the Ferris wheel grounds.

The giant schnauzer reappeared, sat down, and growled at Scarface's prone and limp body. The "Pleasure" wheel ground to a halt and Dad came running, reaching for MV and me. Mom rushed to our side and hugged both of us, crying as she did so. I shook loose and pointed to the top of the wheel, shouting to MV that Arthur had saved us. MV looked up, up to the very top of the rigging, her eyes meeting those of a smiling man who stood atop the Ferris wheel.

I was vaguely conscious that a B&O freight train was screaming down the track next to the Ferris wheel, blowing steam, its whistle blaring. Higgins' carousel accompanied the noise, coming to life, blasting a Christmas melody from its calliope; the "Hallelujah Chorus" filled the air. Arthur looked down, waved to us both, stood straight and tall, his waving red tie making him a bright target in the sky. He gave us a smart salute, and then, in an instant, he was gone.

"He's out of the yard!" MV said, grabbing my shoulders, shaking me hard, grinning from ear to ear.

"Yes! He's out of the yard, and he's up there!" I shouted, pointing to a brilliant star that flashed across the sky.

"Arthur, you're going home and Heaven's the place you'll be," MV said, waving and laughing with joy.

"What are you two talking about? Who was that man on the Ferris wheel? Where did he go?" Mom interrupted, obviously thinking we'd lost our marbles.

MV picked up the slack, turning to Mom and Dad, wide-eyed. "What man?" she asked, "We didn't see any man."

Well, there you have it. MV fibbed to Mom and Dad, without crossing her fingers. But what else could she do? We had absolutely no explanation for Arthur and anything we might have offered would have caused more questions than we could have answered. My parents looked at me with wonder in their eyes and I shook my head, joining and endorsing MV's fib, knowing in my heart it was okay because Mom and Dad would have loved Arthur.

MV turned to me and gave me a bear hug and we watched the shining star move across a cloudless nighttime sky in perfect harmony with the Hallelujah Chorus. Mom watched us and turned her eyes to follow the bright light across the heavens and smiled. I think, in that moment, she knew where the man on the Ferris wheel had gone.

Spiraling downward from the top of the wheel where Arthur had stood was a sheet of white paper. I watched it float lazily down the spine of the Ferris wheel and something told me it was important. Nudging MV, I walked to where the object had landed. MV followed. I picked the paper from the ground and turned it over. The photograph of the Dresser family stared at us.

This time, Lisa Lee was smiling brightly at the camera.

Epilogue

The Christmas of '38 had come to an end. School had resumed and the Maple Avenue Gang was meeting in the Lattice Works beneath our front porch. We reviewed the events of the holiday drama in which we had played starring roles and agreed we had, indeed, given ourselves a swell Christmas present.

RJ Higgins had made bail, but he would eventually be convicted of charges of forgery and intent to defraud, followed by a ten-year prison sentence that lasted only eight years, as he died behind bars.

Scarface was in the same jail but later was transferred to Moundsville State Penitentiary, sentenced to five to ten years on two counts of attempted murder. We realized with apprehension that 1948 would see him set free, sooner if he made parole. We knew, somehow, we would see Scarface again.

John I. Robertson had advised the Grace Methodist Church that the Pullman yard would revert to the Church so that it could build a home for the elderly, and the whole town was cheering the fact that there would be no garbage disposal facility in Paddy Town.

Josh Wenning and Sonny Longsten, the church insisted, would be given a portion of the Pullman yard to house the Pullman Hilton. The Baltimore & Ohio Railroad, at the urging of John I. Robertson, had agreed to give the railroad car to Josh and Sonny; it would be their home and law office. They would each have 50 percent equity, Josh as attorney, Sonny as legal assistant. The Mineral County Library allowed them to keep the book on real estate law, now displayed in a glass case in the Pullman. They proudly shared their quarters with a magnificent and loving giant schnauzer named Briggs. Josh and Sonny flourished in the practice of law, always resplendently dressed with fashions from McCoole's Men's Store.

Mom and Dad were proud of the whole affair, but made MV and me promise we would never again become involved in such antics. We readily agreed as we placed Dad's jacket back in the armoire. Dad insisted that Josh keep his tie and Josh would eventually proudly wear it to the ceremonies inaugurating the new Grace Methodist Home for the Elderly and the opening of the law offices in the Pullman Hilton.

The Maple Avenue Gang had played a significant part in what we thought to be a noble undertaking. We were even featured in a story in *The Paddy Town Daily News*, complete with a picture in front of RJ Higgins' Ferris wheel. Tank, Randy, Jazz Man, Junior, Munch and I were quoted. We all agreed that the indisputable leader and hero of our Christmas adventure of '38 was a girl—a very special girl. A girl we all called "MV".

Oh, and by a unanimous vote, we left out the part about Arthur. Who would have believed us anyway?

The Place, The People, The Reason

This tale of a Paddy Town Christmas is entirely fiction. It encompasses memories of my childhood with my sister and friends on Maple Avenue. The names Mary Virginia, Tank, Munch, Junior, Jazz Man and Randy were the first names or nicknames of my childhood friends, but the story is from my imagination, and my recollections of my hometown of Keyser, West Virginia, once called Paddy Town.

The Pullman yard actually was a collection of only four or five abandoned Pullman cars, not several hundred as depicted in the novel; but they loom large in my memory. I know most of us sneaked a look at the cars from time to time, but we never visited them as a group. I was in several of them and they left an indelible impression on me.

The timeline is also a fabrication; the group depicted actually reached their early teens in the 1950s. I placed the story in the late 1930s to put our activity closer to the Depression, hoboes and the removal of wooden Pullman cars from the nation's railways.

I have taken some leeway with my recounting of Pullman cars and Pullman porters' history. I hope Pullman devotees and historians will forgive me this literary license. I have used Pullman car names that appealed to me and I realize those cars may have been at work during periods other than that which I referenced and certainly would not be in an abandoned graveyard.

I also have written that the abandoned cars in this story were owned by the B&O Railroad. In most instances, however, the Pullman Company actually owned the cars and leased them to railroads.

The real Maple Avenue youngsters I grew up with consisted of good kids who became outstanding men and women—doctors, dentists, naval officers and such. The "Lattice Works" actually existed under our front porch where Mary Virginia and I would play. If memory serves, some neighborhood kids often joined us there.

Dad was a railroad engineer as was Granddad. Granddad ran steam and Dad was at the helm of both steam and diesel engines on the Baltimore & Ohio Railroad. Mom was a sweetheart, holding Mary Virginia and me close to her apron strings. Our parents were hardworking, God-fearing, warm, kind people with the highest ethical standards. They were "salt of the earth" and parented us well.

Arthur, of course, is fiction upon fiction, but I was eager to salute not only railroad Pullman cars but also the men who made them special. Here's to Arthur and all his brothers who rode the rails.

And finally, from MV and me a thank you with much love to our parents. We hope they would have liked this little story about our life on Maple Avenue.

Who knows? Further adventures of the Maple Avenue Gang may be forthcoming.

Acknowledgements

Several people assisted me with the editing of this book. As always, my wife Becky, the love of my life, was the first to read and edit the manuscript. Becky has an incredible editor's eye and is my best and most loving critic.

My good friend Joe Ritchie, former mayor of Newport News, Virginia, was of immeasurable assistance in reviewing my novel, advising me on time sequences and giving me encouragement during many rounds of golf as he hit the ball straight and long. Thanks to Joe and his wife Kathleen for their time, devotion and brilliance as they reviewed my manuscript.

Then came "Jazzman"—whose real name is Fred Riley. Fred and I were close friends in high school in Keyser, West Virginia, (named for William Keyser, a Vice President of the Baltimore & Ohio Railroad).

Jazzman was and is an accomplished musician. He and I actually wrote a few songs together as teenagers, penning the original tune "You Can't Kiss Caroline" for our senior class play. Fred was a much sought-after local musician who went on to earn his doctorate in music, teaching for 30 years and performing around the country with the likes of Bob Hope, Clark Terry and Anna Marie Alberghetti. He is a student of B&O railroad history and his knowledge of "the road" and pictures from the era were enormously helpful in the writing of this novel. You can enjoy more history of the B&O by Googling Fred's web page at *"fluteman70.tripod.com"*.

A very early draft of the story was read and edited by the late and great Steve Gens. Steve was, in my career as a public relations guy, a client and more important, a great friend. Steve passed away just before this book was published. He was incredibly bright and wonderfully funny, utilizing great intellect to educate and entertain. His wife Freddy also edited the book, and she and I remain in touch.

My neighbor Bruce Baumgartner, a retired physician, read the manuscript word-for-word and pointed out to me that such terms as "paralegal" did not exist in the thirties. He also targeted inconsistencies in time and substance that greatly assisted me in writing the story. Without Bruce I would have stumbled more often than I probably have in writing the novel. Please forgive me any inconsistencies of time, grammar, punctuation or excessive imagination.

My high school classmate I so admired and cherished throughout our days of crew cuts and bobby sox, Sharon Wilson, took the completed manuscript and did a final edit. She found out I never met a comma I did not like. Sharon's help was an incredible assist and a great gift to me. Thanks, Sharon. You are the greatest.

The chapters that deal with Harriett Keyser's will are my fabrication and anyone in the legal field may find errors that would not stand up in court.

This book begins my business relationship with Pamela Ovens, whom I have know since she was a child in Charleston, WV, where her mother, Jane Martin, was a television "weather girl"—back before meteorologists handled that gig and when the term "weather girl" was not considered sexist. Her dad, Doug Martin, was a renowned theater star in the community and TV reviewer of local plays and musical performances.

Pamela and her husband Peter Ovens have lived in the Hilton Head Island community for decades. She is the business side of our collaboration, tending to editing, publishing and marketing. Thanks, Pamela, for the opportunity to write and work together.

Glossary

Bad Road A train line rendered useless by some hobos' bad action or crime

Baggage Car Enclosed railroad car that transported excess passenger baggage and mail

Beanery A restaurant catering to railroaders

Bindle Stick A collection of belongings wrapped in cloth and tied to the end of a stick

Boxcar An enclosed railroad car used to transport commercial shipments such as boxes

Bull A railroad policeman

Canned Heat Liquor

Cannonball A fast train

Caller's Office Office in which railroad engineers were called to alert them to their next assignment

Coupler A metal device that connects one train car to another

Cow Crate Sleeper Cars Pullman Sleeper Cars

Covered with the Moon Sleep out in the open

Gondola An open railroad car to transport coal; or a car on a Ferris wheel

Grip A railroader's suitcase

Hawthorne Zep A classic 1930s bicycle manufactured by Montgomery Ward

Hobo A homeless person who often hitched rides on freight trains during the Great Depression

Jackroller One who robs a drunken or sleeping person

Jungle Buzzard A hobo or tramp who preys on his own

Mallet Engine A designation of a certain railroad steam engine class

Maryland State Seal Seals of the State in which a Pullman car was located were placed on the outside of the car

Porter A person employed to carry luggage and tend to the needs and safety of passengers

Rattler A freight train

Road Bed The area between the rails of a railroad line

Rolling Stock Railroad cars, denoting their movement on wheels

Roundhouse A large round building that accommodates a turntable upon which locomotive engines were placed in order to easily move them into bays for servicing their various moving parts

Royal Blue Line Upscale passenger trains on the B&O Railroad

Schwinn Camelback Classic bicycle of the 1930s

Tanker Car An enclosed railroad car designed to carry liquids

Toddy A glass of liquor or a mixed drink

Tokay Blanket Drinking alcohol to stay warm

Turn A railroader's description of a day's work; running an engine to a certain location and then turning to journey back to its home rail yard

Walking Dandruff Lice

Watchman Railroad employee assigned to railroad crossings; the job consisted of telling pedestrians and automobile drivers when they could and could not cross the rails

Yegg A traveling professional thief or burglar

Z Tower A tower on the B&O line near Keyser, WV where signals were given to engineers that directed them to their assigned tracks; tracks were switched at this location, allowing movement of trains from one track to another

A Brief Word about Pullman Cars

Pullman Cars were essentially hotel rooms on wheels, designed to bring comfort to the American railroad traveler. The Pullman car originated in 1867. The fleet was in existence into the late 1960s, when competition from automobile and airplane transportation made luxury train travel too costly and time-consuming.

During the one hundred years Pullman cars rode the rails, hundreds of thousands enjoyed their amenities. Many of the wood, steel, and aluminum cars exist to this day in museums. If one wishes to go back to that time in history there are a number of companies that offer excursions on refurbished Pullman cars.

The Pullman porters were largely black. These incredibly articulate men are credited with advancing the country's black middle class, beginning with their service shortly after the Civil War and into the turn of the Century. Their story is an important part of America's history, encompassing entrepreneurialism, labor unions, and elegant travel.

Many Pullman porters, as depicted here, worked four hundred hours in a month's time and many left the Pullman Company to continue their education. Some received law degrees and returned to Pullman service because there was little work for black lawyers. Arthur Boreman illustrates that sad fact.

The rich history of the Pullman Company and Pullman porters is one that I urge my readers, particularly young adults, to explore. It is a remarkable adventure—of which the Maple Avenue Gang was privileged to carve out just a tiny slice.

The Maple Avenue Gang, photograph courtesy of Jerry Pifer.

The gentleman in the white coveralls is the engineer, my
grandfather, Benjamin Franklin Ryan. The young man second
from right in the cap is my father, William Donaldson Ryan, a
crew member on this train who also became a railroad engineer.

My dad preparing to leave the house for his turn on the road. MV
and I look on with love and admiration, I in my railroader's cap.

About the Author

Charlie Ryan lives on Hilton Head Island, South Carolina with his wife Becky and their Maltese, Amalfi. *The Pullman Hilton, A Christmas Mystery*, is his second novel, following publication of *Dead Men's Clubs*, a story of golf, death and redemption, available in bookstores and online.

Charlie was a television news anchor and news director before founding Charles Ryan Associates, a marketing firm with a business base in West Virginia, Virginia, and Washington, D.C. He sold his marketing firm of 33 years in 2007 and became the Founding Dean of the Graduate School of Business at the University of Charleston in Charleston, WV. He now concentrates on writing, golf, and community involvement in Sea Pines Plantation on Hilton Head Island.

Charlie's Maple Avenue friends stay in touch, along with the 1958 Keyser High School graduating class, through Facebook and collective e-mails coordinated by classmate Eddie Taylor, to whom the Class of '58 owes much gratitude.